1

Throw Me to the Wolves

ISBN: 978-1-365-69372-4

3

For my mother, who always believed in me

And to Shia LaBeouf: I did not let my dreams be dreams

4

<u>One</u>

"C'mon kid. We're close."

He had said those words hundreds of times in the last month. But at 29,000 feet, through the blistering cold and the unfiltered rays of the unforgiving sun, the words had a different meaning. Up here, they were always close to something—mainly death. But finally, after a struggle few can comprehend, they reached their final goal.

The goal in question was the summit of Mount Everest. And for Blue Jennings, this wasn't the first time he had made this journey.

But even though he had been there before, the summit always had a different feeling. The environment was similar no doubt: the endless entombment of his body and equipment in ice, the burning of his fingers, toes, eyes, ears, and even organs as the cold ensconced him, the constant laboring of breath as his lungs screamed for air— all these were familiar feelings. But as Blue trudged up the last few feet of snow, a sense of invincibility washed over him. It wasn't the first time he had felt this.

Blue stopped just shy of the summit and peered behind him. Just below was one of his clients, 23-year-old Robert Newcomb. This was the kid's first attempt at Everest and he was about to accomplish something nearly impossible. Blue was proud he was the one leading him to the top.

With shaking hands, Blue reached up towards his face and tugged away at his oxygen mask. The ice had accumulated around his beard, but after a few attempts, he managed to rip the crusty tool from his head. The cold stung at his exposed skin, but for the first time in months, he didn't feel it.

"Rob…that's it. Keep pushing!"

Robert stumbled in front of him, but Blue caught him. "I can't…carry you now kid…" he panted out. "You're close."

"Not bad…for a poker player," Robert said, smiling. He was spent. Blue knew it. Getting down the mountain would be very hard for Robert, but Blue would worry about that later.

He gave him a pat on the back. "It's all you."

Standing on the summit of Mount Everest, one could almost grasp the curvature of the Earth. When coming home, Blue Jennings always found this his hardest sight to describe. Some parts of this view he wanted to keep to himself because, well, he had earned it. But a sense of duty towards others made him an unselfish man. Except on one occasion.

Blue shed his sunglasses and gazed longingly out across the Himalayan peaks. He closed his eyes and listened to the snapping of the Buddhist prayer flags in the wind. It was utter peace.

Robert also removed his oxygen mask and breathed in the thin air. "If my tears wouldn't freeze," he said, "I'd cry right now."

Blue laughed and pulled a camera from his backpack. "You did well kid…now smile."

Blue snapped some victory poses of Robert, then took a few of the peaks below him.

"The roof…of the world…" he panted to the kid.

Blue would never take the view for granted. As he saw it, the last nonviolent place on Earth was this very summit, a space no larger than a picnic table. Voices from a crowd behind him, however, reminded Blue that it was no longer the most peaceful.

There was a time when Everest wasn't a tourist attraction for the rich. Only the best climbers in the world could tackle this mountain, and even then, most of them couldn't. Now, all it took was finding an experienced guide—and a hundred thousand dollars, of course—and the dream could be bought.

Most of these tourists disgusted Blue. But then again, he'd be out of a job if it weren't for them.

He imagined the traffic jam of people stacked up at the Hillary Step, the final obstacle to reaching the summit, and he tried his best to enjoy his final moments in solitude on the ceiling of Earth.

"Fourth time's the charm, huh slick?" a muffled voice called out from behind him.

7

Blue put the camera down and saw a woman ambling with ease up to the summit. Her long-limbed, bony features, plus the lack of any kind of oxygen equipment, gave her away immediately.

"'Bout time, Domino," he heaved out. "I was getting worried…"

She put her hand on his shoulder. "Don't wear yourself out, big guy," she said through a circular wired-mask.

Domino had been Blue's climbing partner for the last eight years. When Blue founded his climbing company, Alliance Expeditions, she was his first choice at helping him run his team. Despite her spidery figure, the woman had physical and mental strength matchless to any man he had ever met. Throughout their work relationship, he watched her get teased for being a woman in a so-called man's world. But it never fazed her; she thrived in this type of environment. Domino had already proven herself climbing Everest without supplemental oxygen, and she was about to prove herself again.

For the third time.

"You got a crowd headed your way," she reminded him.

Blue nodded. He was too busy staring out at the peaks below. A slap on the shoulder courtesy of Domino broke his concentration.

"Hey, stay focused," she said sharply. "Don't let that mind wander."

She was right. The hardest part about the climb was actually descending. The brain suffers from a drop in oxygen, and mistakes are made easily as a result. And when easy mistakes are made up here, there are no second chances.

Robert staggered over to them. "I couldn't…have done it…without you guys." He bent down with hands on his knees and coughed violently.

Domino grabbed his shoulders, pulling him back up to eye level. "You all right, kid?"

Robert nodded. "Just a little winded."

Domino fastened the oxygen mask back around his face and checked his levels. "You're low on O2," she said.

"I am?" he said, surprised.

Blue took a look for himself. "You must've accidently touched the valve." It was a common error but also one of the most punishing.

Robert definitely looked confused. He was reaching a perilous state, and Blue realized he needed to get down immediately.

"Listen, kid. Tenzing is posted down at the Hillary Step. He's got an extra O2 tank."

Tenzing was Blue's Sirdar, or head Sherpa. One cannot climb Everest without help from a Sherpa; their superhuman strength and endurance surpasses that of any climber who has ever lived.

"Right." Robert glanced one last time at the awe-inspiring view, then headed down.

Blue watched him bump headlong into a crowd of excited climbers nearing the summit. He knew he should go down with him, but he also wanted to enjoy what might, as always, be his last time up here.

"Well, at least one of our clients made it," Domino said underbreath. They had started out with two others, but both of them had decided to give up upon reaching Camp Four.

Blue shrugged his shoulders. "Maybe one day."

A Southern voice drawled out from a group of approaching climbers. "If the creek don't rise!"

Blue didn't need to turn around to know that the "Cowboy of Everest," or so he styled himself, had caught up to them.

"Alex Greene. Where've you been?" Blue smiled falsely and they shook hands.

Greene bowed to Domino. "Howdy, gorgeous!" he said with extra Southern charm.

Domino, too tired to put Greene in his place, just returned the nod to make him go away.

Greene breathed in the crisp air. "Lemme learn y'all sumthin', Blue, this one nearly kilt me." He looked out across the vast, white region beneath him. "Took longer than a month of Sundays, but goddamn, always worth it."

"That's a new one," Domino mumbled.

Greene's climbing company was fairly new. He had begun just a few seasons after Blue, and this was only his second time on the summit.

"Y'all got any knickknacks to leave up here?" Greene asked, reaching into his pack.

"Not this time," Blue said.

Greene presented a photograph to Blue. The picture was of himself as a kid, with none other than the first man to summit Everest: Edmund Hillary.

"Met him when I was a young'un. I told him I would run with the big dogs one day." He dug a small hole with his gloved hand, then carefully placed the photo in the snow. "Wish I told him I was gonna summit twice."

Nausea suddenly slapped Blue in the face. He bent down, hands on his knees, and sucked hard for air.

Domino came over and tenderly put Blue Jennings' oxygen mask back around his face. She started on checking the O2 levels when Blue's radio crackled to life.

"Mr. Jennings—need—down—now—"

Blue straightened up, seizing the radio clipped to his jacket. "Say again?"

"The—step—get here—now—"

"I think that's Tenzing," Domino assumed.

The radio squawked. "Mr. Newcomb—no good—"

"Rob?" Blue grew alarmed. He studied all the faces in the oncoming crowd. Something was wrong. He could feel it.

"I'm going down," Blue said to Domino.

"I hope he's all right," she offered.

"Me too."

Blue began to hike down, but an urge to take one last look at the summit overcame him. He saw Greene taking pictures with some of his clients. He heard people laughing noisily, hugging and high-fiving one another. Someone tossed a candy bar wrapper over the side.

The new Everest, he thought.

The radio hissed to life. "Mr. Jennings!" Tenzing yelled, panic-stricken.

Blue keyed the radio. "Coming."

After a few tense minutes of pushing past the flow of climbers, Blue was standing at the peak of the Hillary Step. He gazed downward and followed an assembly of climbers gathered around a lump in the snow. Grabbing a free rope, Blue clipped in and began the descent.

When he reached the bottom, Tenzing intercepted him before he could reach the attraction.

"It's no good, Mr. Jennings!" he said over and over. "It's no good!"

Blue moved him aside and raced over to what he could now see was a body.

Robert Newcomb. He was sprawled on his back, his face completely mashed into a bloody pulp.

"Jesus Christ," Blue managed. He fell to his knees in the snow and grasped one of Robert's lifeless hands.

"What happened?" he said without looking up.

Tenzing explained frantically that when Robert was halfway down the Step, a large chunk of ice broke loose above him. He had looked up just in time for it to break his face apart.

Blue shook his head.

"I'm sorry, Mr. Jennings." Tenzing placed a hand on his shoulder.

Reaching into his backpack, Blue removed a tarp and draped it over Robert's body. There was no way to get him back to base camp. He would remain here, at the bottom of the Hillary Step, forever consigned to the slopes of Everest.

Climbers continued to pass them by, callous to the situation occurring a few feet away. After a long time, Blue stood up.

"I gotta make the call," he told Tenzing, then stiffly began to work his way back down.

Two

Sitting around 26,000 feet, Camp Four—the "Death Zone"—was the last stop for climbers before the final push towards the summit. As the last on the way up, it was also first on the way down. Consequently, Camp Four came with a slew of emotions—elation, exhaustion, defeat, and desperation for a few. But as Blue plodded into the camp, he felt none of these. In fact, he felt nothing at all. Stonefaced, he entered the communications tent.

An older woman with sandy blonde hair sat huddled by a stove. When she saw Blue, she stood up immediately and embraced him.

"Tenzing radioed me about Robert," she said softly. "I'm so sorry, Blue-bird."

Blue Jennings had all but collapsed in her arms. "Just one of those things, El," he muttered.

Eleanor Abby had been helping climbers communicate with each other as long as Blue had been scaling Everest. She was a good-looking woman in her 50's and was in better shape than he would likely ever be.

She pulled away. "Your other clients are resting in the next tent over. I don't think they know. Do you want me to—"

"I gotta make the call, El," Blue blurted.

"Right," she sighed. "The phones aren't working too well up here. I'm sorry, Blue-bird, but I think it's best to wait and have someone at base camp do it. It's getting dark soon."

The phone malfunction did not surprise Blue. They never worked when they were needed.

Blue removed a chunk of ice from his oxygen mask. "It has to be me," he said flatly. "He was my client."

Camp Three was 2,000 feet below, but navigating through the slopes, especially with nightfall nearing, could take hours.

"Radio Jevel at Camp Three and tell him I'll be down soon," he told Eleanor Abby.

She shook her head in disapproval. She had known Blue too long; there was no way to sway him. She told him to wait as she searched the tent.

El produced an extra oxygen tank and gifted it to Blue. "You'll need this," she said.

Blue thanked her and exchanged the old tank for the new. He set the O2 flow at 2.5 liters per minute and cleared out the last of the ice encrusted around the regulator.

Before he left the tent, he turned to El. "I'll be all right," he said.

She smiled. "I know."

From the crest of the Geneva Spur, Blue watched the night cloak the mountain. Clouds had begun to roll in, but there was just enough space in the sky for him to view the stars. They winked down in a speckling, sparkling pattern of celestial warmth.

And then they were gone, disappearing behind the haze of thick, freezing moisture. Blue kicked his crampons into the blackened rock, then continued his descent.

He was aware that the weather is the only factor that decided the climb. One could train one's whole life to tackle this beast, but no amount of preparation could ready one for the punitive wrath of Mother Nature.

Which is why most deaths happen on the mountain. Blue knew of many climbers and guides who underestimated what a storm could do at these heights. The sense of immortality is shattered when confronted with the elements, little oxygen, and no help.

By then it's too late.

Blue finished his descent of the Geneva Spur just as visibility began to fog. The cold was augmenting and his energy was diminishing; he hadn't eaten in three days, mainly because of the digestive setback the body suffers at such altitudes. Fatigue ate at his heels, but he kicked it off with a focus only cultivated through years of mental discipline.

Robert was his responsibility. He had to make the call.

He clicked on the beam of his headlamp and stumbled in drunkenly towards his next obstacle: the Yellow Band. The incline was steep and required over 300 feet of rope to scale. But the unrelenting flurries kept it obscured.

Blue felt his eyes burning in the icy gale. He crouched among the rocks and probed desperately for the rope. Being stuck between two camps in the middle of a storm surely meant death and he knew it. His breathing hastened with this realization, but he quickly calmed himself. Panicking only worsens things.

"Hey!"

He thought he heard a voice call into the night. He thought it the wind, but soon realized it was not his imagination. The headlamp of a fellow climber bobbed up toward him.

"You lost?" the mountaineer shouted over the gusts.

The beam blinded Blue, but he could discern that the climber was a man about ten years his senior in a thick carmine jacket. Squinting into the light, Blue managed a reply.

"The rope," he chattered.

The man handed over the twine and Blue took it. He hunched over, shielding his chest from the wind, and tied loose knot. When he looked up to thank him, the man had already vanished into the flurry.

Even an experienced guide like Blue can occasionally find himself lost on a familiar mountain. Everest changes every season; perpetual avalanches and constant snowfall are always altering the routes. Add the chaos of night and a heavy storm and it will always mean trouble, experienced be damned.

Upon finishing his descent of the Yellow Band, Blue untied himself before attempting to chart his route. Down was the obvious direction, but no way in hell he'd wander off a ledge. He racked his memory for the direction of Camp Three, then pressed on.

He no longer felt the frigid gas from the oxygen around his mouth. He knew, if he set the flow correctly, that he should still have a few hours left. He stopped amidst the snow pellets and checked the regulator.

Instead of the 2.5 liters-per-minute flow he thought he had set, he had accidently turned the valve to 3.5. He cursed his hypoxia and shed the weight of the empty tank.

"Keep moving!" he pushed himself aloud. "You gotta make the call!"

Just then the haze dispersed long enough for him to see the tent city of Camp Three flapping in the wind. A gust of wind knocked him on his side. Drained, he laid in the snow for a period of time. But determination was branded inside of him. A client was dead and Robert his responsibility. Blue had to keep moving.

He pulled himself to his feet and continued. His legs heaved as if burdened with weights. His lungs panged with fire, crying out in the thin atmosphere. The tents didn't seem to be getting closer; he felt he was walking on an icy treadmill.

Then, through the haze of the headlamp, he saw a figure waving its arms, coming towards him in the snow. Blue sighed in relief when he realized it was Jevel Williams.

"Blue Jennings!" he shouted into the night.

Blue straightened his posture, feeling a newfound energy wash over him. He walked closer, not sure if what he was seeing was real. But there stood Jevel, the self-styled "Comedian of Everest."

"Jevel, is that you?" Blue asked wearily.

"That better not be a black-man-in-the-dark joke!" he yelled in the screaming wind.

Blue smiled behind the mask. "Good to see you, buddy," he called, not sure if he was heard.

Jevel swung an arm his arm around Blue's waist. "El radioed down and said you were comin'! I expected you hours ago!"

Blue acknowledged him with a nod. He simply responded with, "Everest."

Jevel patted him on the back. "C'mon!"

He directed him through the snowfall and into a tent nestled in the middle of camp. He pulled back the flap and shoved Blue in.

"Close the door!" a bundled fellow bellowed from a sleeping bag.

"How many times I gotta tell ya, Vince? It's a tent, there aren't any goddamn doors." Jevel reached over for a cup on a stove and handed it to Blue. "Just melted some snow. You better hydrate, I don't wanna have you pissin' brown all night."

Blue took off his oxygen mask along with his goggled glasses and sipped on the water.

Jevel continued. "She told me about your client, the kid. I'm sorry, my man. Shit jus' ain't right."

"I need a phone, Jevel," Blue said. "I need to notify the family." He turned to the man named Vince.

"Right," Vince replied. He sat up and rummaged through a duffle bag and produced a satellite phone. "Not sure you're gonna get much of a signal in this weather."

Blue grabbed the phone anyway. For a second, he just sat staring at it, his hands still quivering from the cold.

"All right, Vince, get up," Jevel ordered. "Let's give the man some privacy."

Vince reluctantly slunk from the warmth of the sleeping bag and threw on his boots. "Take your time," he told Blue before crawling out of the tent.

Jevel gave him an encouraging nod. He had been friends with Blue for years, and knew he had never made this kind of call before.

"I'm sorry, brother," he said with a rare gentleness. Then he left Blue to himself.

Blue Jennings painstakingly loosened the straps of his backpack and pulled it around. Riffling through the pack, he found his spiral-bound notebook and began flipping through the pages.

Ever since starting Alliance Expeditions, Blue had kept a volume on all of his clients. Most of it was just contact information, addresses and phone numbers. But every once in a while, Blue would jot a few notes about the climbers—where they traveled from or what occupation they held. He liked to remember people, especially the good ones.

When he got to Robert's page, however, something caught his eye. Next to the emergency contact info, he had written

Remember to take $100 off climbing fee

A smile crept on Blue's face and he fought to bottle his sadness. He had forgotten about their first night in Nepal when they played heads-up Texas hold'em in the lobby. The kid had given him a run for his money.

He took a deep breath, then started to dial.

Three

Blue awoke to a chill stinging his unshaven face. He sat up quickly and looked to the entrance of the tent. The flaps had been pulled back. There someone stood, staring down at him.

"Good morning, handsome man," the individual said.

It was Domino. Blue rubbed his eyes and reached for a mug of liquefied snow.

"What time is it?" he asked groggily.

"Afternoon, technically," she said. "C'mon, let's talk."

Blue had fallen asleep still wearing his boots and skull cap. He removed the covers and slowly rose to his feet. He finished off the water and stumbled outside.

Emerging from the tent, he winced in the sun. He reached into his jacket and threw on his sunglasses.

"The kid's dead," he said stiffly.

"I know," she said, standing before him. Blue hadn't seen her face this exposed in a few weeks. He forgot how beautiful her features were: the short sable hair rounding her ears, the pronounced features of her face, and of course those lancing amber eyes. Sometimes, when the light hit them right, a hint of gold streaked through them.

"You make the call?" she asked, breaking his concentration.

Blue nodded.

"How'd it go?"

"How's the rest of the team?" Blue said, avoiding the question.

"Fine," she replied. "They're working their way down now. Tenzing and Greene will be taking them the rest of the way."

Blue gazed aimlessly at the frozen peaks above. "I can do it. Greene doesn't need to pick up my slack."

"I know, slick," she said. "But something has come up. For the both of us."

Blue looked at her. "What are you talking about?"

"Well, when I got to Camp Four last night, a man was there waiting for me—well, for you actually."

"What? Like a client?"

"Not exactly," she said. "This guy looked like he knew what he was doing."

"What did he say?" Blue pressed.

"Just that there was someone at base camp who really needed to talk to you. And that it was extremely imperative that you do so immediately."

"What else?" he said, curtly.

"That was it."

Blue stood for a minute contemplating the news. "I need to see about my team—our team."

"The team is fine, Blue," she responded. "They're in good hands with Tenzing."

"They didn't pay to be in Tenzing's hands, Dom," he shot back. "They're our clients and it's my job to make sure they're safe."

Domino sighed. "Robert's death is not on you," she said, putting her hands on her hips, the classic Domino stance.

"What?"

"It's not your fault, slick—this is Everest. People die every year. And Robert knew the risks."

"Yeah, well I should have been there. I sent him down and I should have been there with him." He looked out into the Himalayas.

Domino placed a hand on Blue's shoulder. "You're a great leader, Blue. And an even better man. But right now I think there's someone else who needs our help."

Blue shook her off. "Well, you can tell this guy to shove his request up his ass. I've got other people to take care of."

"Tell him yourself," she said sorely. "He's walking into camp right now."

Blue looked up and saw a man in a bright red jacket heading directly towards them.

"That's him?" Blue asked, trying to remember why he thought the man looked familiar.

"Yup."

"All right. Let's get this over with."

The man was tall, just over six feet, and walked with a slight limp. His broad shoulders made his head look too small for his body. A dark, rosy beard consumed most of his face and reached down to his sternum. With the vivid cover he sported, Blue thought he could probably spot him from base camp if he stood on the summit. He seemed intimidating but smiled big when he reached them.

"Are you Mr. Jennings?" he asked. "Blue Jennings?"

"That's right," Blue said coldly.

"The name's Dave Redding," he said, offering a hand. "It's a pleasure to meet you."

Blue ignored this offer, staring blankly at him.

"I heard you lost a client," Redding said, retracting his hand. "Tough break. I'm sorry for your loss."

"I need to get back to my team," Blue responded angrily. "So will you please tell me, Mr. Redding, what is so important?"

"I'll cut right to it, then," he said, removing his thick Oakleys. He needled Blue with sharp, determined eyes. "I've been hired to come retrieve you. There's some men at base camp who'd like to speak with you."

"About what?"

"A job. That's all I can say."

Blue scoffed. "I already have one, if you haven't noticed."

"I can see that," Redding replied. "But the climbing season is almost up. And pretty soon you're going to be without one. I—well, the individual that we represent— needs your help."

Blue shook his head. "Why can't this wait?"

"Because the clock is ticking," Redding answered. "The job is time-sensitive."

"Who is this person you represent?" Domino cut in.

Redding grinned. "A very powerful person."

"And you can't tell us?" Blue spat.

"Mr. Jennings, all of your and Ms. Domino's questions will be answered. All you have to do is come with me."

Blue didn't respond. For a few tense seconds, the two men stared directly at each other. Blue Jennings did not like being told what to do, especially by strangers.

"Will you excuse us for a minute?" Domino cut in, taking Blue by the arm.

Redding smiled warmly once more. "Of course."

She led Blue to the other side of the tent and out of earshot.

"Who the hell does this Redding guy think he is?" Blue growled.

"Listen," Domino began, "I know this is going to sound bizarre, but I really think we should head down with this guy."

"What?" Blue exclaimed. "What are you talking about?"

"I thought I recognized him last night at Camp Four, but I wasn't sure it was him until now."

Blue stared at her, angry with himself for being slightly intrigued.

Domino continued. "You ever heard of the story about the ship that sunk in the Arctic Ocean sometime in the early 80's?"

"Maybe," Blue thought aloud. "I'm not sure."

"Well, he and the rest of his crew got stranded out there near Siberia. Something like five or six months they were out there. He was apparently the only one to make it out alive."

"Are you serious?" Blue said.

"Yeah."

"And that's the same guy?"

"It's the same guy."

Blue took a deep breath and exhaled harshly.

"Look, I don't feel any better about it than you do," she said, "but I really think we should go down to base camp and see what these people have to say."

"I don't know, Dom…"

"After we talk to them, we can rendezvous with the team and take them the rest of the way. We can always make good with Tenzing later; he knows we're good for it."

Blue stood in silence, contemplating his next move. He would be lying if he said he wasn't mildly curious about what someone would possibly want with him, a Mount Everest guide.

"All right, Dom," he said finally. "But let's make it quick."

Four

The trek down to base camp took a grueling day and a half. Many times Blue and Domino had to stop and give their bodies a break. Redding said nothing about the matter, but his body language betrayed annoyance.

The south face of the mountain led into a valley called the Western Cwm. At 20,000 feet, one of the scariest routes was actually just above base camp. The Khumbu Icefall was the first real hurdle of Everest. Jagged, delicate slivers of ice interposed the section of the route with bottomless crevasses beneath. Connecting the opposite sides of the chasms were aluminum ladders allowing climbers to inch their way across.

The trickiest part for Blue was having to watch his feet as he balanced precariously over the steps. Feet placement was key, for the spiky metal crampon spears could cause an easy slip down into thin air.

Base camp was a less arduous course. This region of Everest was also the hottest, with temperatures soaring into a heat reminiscent of a Florida summer.

Blue and Domino shed their jackets, tying them around their waists as the three of them approached the perimeter. They followed Redding through a maze of tents until finally, he stopped at one of the fanciest bivouacs Blue had ever seen.

Redding opened the tent flap. "After you," he said to them.

Blue hesitated before Domino ushered him in. When he got inside, three men in tan jackets around a rectangular fold-up table eyed them closely. After a moment of silence, Blue spoke first.

"I'm Blue Jennings," he said.

A middle-aged man in the center stood up. He was short and shaven, and he smiled with faux sincerity.

"Mr. Jennings!" he said. "You're the man behind Alliance Expeditions, correct?"

"That's right."

"Excellent!" The man walked over quickly. "I'm Mr. Colby. At the table are my associates, Mr. Young and Mr. Broadway." He pointed to a man in his late sixties who dragged on an unfiltered cigarette and a younger man in his early twenties who fiddled with a guitar.

He then stuck his hand out to Blue. "Thank you for coming down on such short notice."

Blue studied his hand, then reluctantly shook it.

Colby turned his attention to Domino. "And you must be…"

"Domino," she said simply. "The *woman* behind Alliance Expeditions."

"She's my business partner. Dom helped me start the company," Blue explained, wondering why he had to in the first place.

Colby nodded. He strolled over to a steaming pot in the corner of the tent. He poured two cups and walked back over. "It's coffee," he said. "I'm sorry—I seem to be out of cream and sugar."

Blue held his hand out in front of the cup, but Domino shrugged, accepting the offer.

"All right, Mr. Colby, what exactly is so important?" Blue demanded.

The man smiled once more. "You're from Seattle, right?"

"Yeah."

"So you are familiar with Governor Heather Stone?"

Blue contemplated for a second. "Yeah," he recalled, "isn't she running for president?"

"She is." Colby sipped on Blue's unwanted coffee and leaned back against the table.

"Do you all work for her?"

Colby nodded. "Yes. We represent her, I guess you could say."

"Okay, I guess my next question is why has the Governor of Washington sent you to the base camp of

Everest to come retrieve me?" Blue folded his arms and
glanced from Mr. Young to Mr. Broadway, then back to
Mr. Colby.

Colby put the coffee down. "Mr. Jennings, Ms.
Domino, what I am about to tell you cannot leave this
room."

Blue shuffled his feet uncomfortably and glanced
back at Domino. "Fine," he said.

Colby cleared his throat. "A few days ago, Governor
Stone's husband, Dr. Stone, went missing. He and his
three-man team were working in the polar region just north
of Alaska. His plan was to spend a month at a research
station conducting experiments and what have you. Two
days ago he was supposed to fly back to Washington and
contact the Governor. But there's been no word from him
or anyone on his team."

The man to Colby's left took a hard puff of his
cigarette and started slicking back his thinning, white hair.

"Mr. Young," Colby said with a turn of his head,
"care to elaborate?"

"The plane they traveled in was owned and piloted
by Dr. Stone," he said in a gravelly voice. "Satellite imaging
of the research station shows a hangar at the compound,
but we can't see inside. We're not sure if the plane is still
there or even if they made it to their destination at all." He
took another hit, a thick cloud of smoke billowing around
his face. "Needless to say, this is quite the problem."

Blue took a breath.

Colby continued. "Now there is something we do
know: either he's very much dead or he's very much alive.
And the longer we wait the better chance our dilemma will
go public."

"Wait," Blue said. "You're worried about his absence
being leaked to the press? Shouldn't word already be out
that he's missing?"

"Mr. Jennings, there is something you need to
understand about politics," Young said. "The United States
is literally *weeks* away from the Democratic Presidential
Primary. Governor Stone is the frontrunner for the
Democratic Party. Do you think a missing husband is going
to help her chances?"

Colby held out his hand. "I think what Mr. Young is trying to say is that the well-being of Dr. Stone is critical to her political situation."

Young leaned back and puffed irritably on the cigarette.

Blue glanced at Domino and let out a slight laugh. "Listen, I don't know who you guys think we are, but we are certainly not detectives. I'm not sure where we fit into all of this."

"Mr. Jennings. You are not a detective, you're an outdoorsman," Colby clarified. "You are an adventurer in hostile environments. A man who has summited Everest as much as you no doubt knows of the punishing effects the cold can have on a person, am I right?"

"Yes, but—"

"And you are not afraid of death, or even to see what ensues because of it. That's a valuable trait, Mr. Jennings."

Blue stopped him. "All right, I see where you're going with this. But I'm sure there are better people for the job."

"There are." This time it was Mr. Broadway, who never looked up from the guitar. "But if the government found out, her political status would be compromised."

Colby stepped closer to Blue and Domino. "If anything, look at it as a human being in need. We already have a team, but it's not strong enough. Lives are at stake here. You can choose to be a part of it and maybe make a difference, or you can read about what could have been in next week's newspaper."

"So what do you suppose I do about my clients?" Blue retorted. "I'm still in the middle of an expedition, if you haven't noticed."

Colby nodded. "The timing is poor, this we know. But I can assure you we wouldn't have flown across the world if you weren't one of our last resorts."

"You said you have a team together?" Domino asked.

"It's a good team," said Colby. "But besides Mr. Redding, none of them have much experience in dealing with a life-and-death crisis such as this. Not to mention in a setting as grueling as the Arctic can be."

"I've never been to the Arctic," Blue said, "but I'm pretty sure we are talking about two different environments."

"With a common ground of ice and cold," Colby pressed.

Young leaned forward in his chair. "The North Polar region is a mental game, Mr. Jennings. Everest is a physical and emotional challenge." He snubbed the cigarette out in an ashtray in front of him, but kept his eyes on Blue. "If you are worried about the danger, I can assure you there aren't any mountains to fall off."

"I'm not afraid," Blue shot back immediately. "But two days ago I lost a client. A kid. The family is going to want answers, and it isn't going to look good on me or my company if I just up and disappear."

"Yes, the kid. Robert Newcomb from Star City, correct?" Colby said, turning to Mr. Broadway for confirmation, who nodded slowly in agreement.

Blue stared back in astonishment. "How do you know this?"

"We find people," said Mr. Broadway, "and we fix the situation."

"Robert Newcomb's family will be taken care of," Mr. Colby added. "I'll even see that his body is brought down from the mountain and sent home for a proper burial."

Blue removed his cap and raked his fingers through his long, matted hair. "I just don't know. It's a lot to take in so quickly."

"I know, Mr. Jennings. But maybe this will help." Colby dug into his coat pocket, and pulled out a folded check. "Governor Stone takes care of her friends."

Blue took the check and opened it slowly. "My God." He closed it again.

"Not so fast." Domino snatched the check from his hand and unfolded it. She gaped in disbelief.

"This is almost what we've made since starting the company," Blue said to her under his breath.

"So what do you say, Mr. Jennings? Can we count on your support?" Colby said, grinning. "Oh, and I suppose I should be asking you too, Ms. Domino."

Blue looked at Domino, who nodded at him with wide eyes.

"All right, Mr. Colby. We have a deal. Only if you keep your word about Robert."

Colby glanced behind him at Mr. Broadway. For the first time, he looked up from the guitar. He nodded once, then returned to his work.

"It will be done," Colby responded. "You have my word."

They shook on it.

"So what happens now?" Blue asked.

"A helicopter will be arriving shortly to take you two and Mr. Redding into a town not far from here," Colby explained. "From there, a series of flights will take you to a port in Alaska where a boat will take you the rest of the way."

"And what about you three?" said Domino. "Will you all be joining us on this expedition?"

"We are waiting on one more person for the team," Colby replied. "But we have business elsewhere."

There was a long pause. A breeze coming off the mountain gently swayed the tent inward.

"Any other questions?" Colby asked.

Domino and Blue shook their heads.

"Good," he said. "Now get out of my tent."

The duo obeyed and walked back out to the incredible view of the towering Himalayas.

"Don't suppose you want to cash that check in and disappear, huh?" Domino said when they were out of earshot.

"Not sure I want to test these people," replied Blue. He donned his glasses and stared out across the camp at Redding, who sat on a rock sharpening a large knife.

"Who do you think they're waiting for?" Domino said.

Blue shrugged. "Jevel, if we're lucky."

"I don't think we're that lucky."

"Are you sure you're up for this?"

"You know I pull my own weight, slick." Domino
slapped him on the back. "We're a team, remember?"
"I know."
"Or should I say, 'business partners'?"
Blue smiled. Somewhere off in the distance, the
thumping of a helicopter's rotors echoed across the valley.
And then it begun.

Five

The comforts of a normal lifestyle were never
something Blue Jennings felt he needed. For most of his
life, he lived in either tents or hostels, traveling and
climbing around the world since he graduated high school.
Unlike Domino, he didn't come from wealth. He
never had much, but he never needed much. Material
possessions meant nothing to him, but experiences meant
everything. Objects break, he thought, but memories go on.
Maybe that's why he was so attracted to the people
of Nepal. Blue found them a very happy bunch. The
Sherpas he climbed with were some of the nicest
individuals Blue had ever met. They were also deeply
religious. Before making the drive to the Summit from base
camp, the Sherpas perform a religious ceremony to the
mountain asking for safe passage. Blue was never a spiritual
man, but he always enjoyed the sacral tradition. Sherpas
believe it is their duty to help climbers survive on Everest.
In his experience, Blue never once saw a Sherpa leave a
man behind. They would lay their lives on the line for a
complete stranger. They were delighted to do so.
As Blue lied on his back in the small hotel room, he
thought of Tenzing and the other Sherpas he had
encountered. Would they depart as he did to help a
stranger? Most certainly. But would they leave their group
behind to do so? This was the question that ate at Blue.
On the left wall of the room were two long,
rectangular windows he had left open. Outside on the
avenue below, a festival of sorts was going on. The
townspeople danced through the street, carousing loudly.

He had asked for a room with a view of the Himalayas. He loved how the mountains looked, especially at night. Tonight they were exceptionally beautiful, peaks jutting into the stark, black sky and a thousand glistening stars. The moon was full behind a tall summit that half blocked its milky light.

Blue sat up and stared into the sky's eye. A draft softly swayed the musty curtains and lapped his freshly shaven cheeks. He closed his eyes and thought about Robert. The guilt began to well. He was beginning to second guess his deal with Colby when he heard a knock at his door.

Blue waited, pretending he wasn't there. But the knock came again.

"Come in!" he shouted.

"It's locked!" a voice answered.

Sighing bitterly, Blue stood and ambled sluggishly to the door. He flung it open. Leaning against the frame was Domino.

"Hey, handsome man," she said.

He rubbed his eyes. "Howdy, pretty lady."

Domino studied his face, his newly cut mustache. "You clean up well."

Blue smiled. "Not joining in on the festivities?" he said, nodding toward the street below.

"Nope."

"Not my style either."

"Besides, I thought we would have some 'festivities' of our own," she replied. She held up her hand; pinched between her fingers were two joints. "I think this is more along the lines of our style, huh?"

Blue laughed. "Well, I'll be damned."

"I bought them off that kid who sold us that shitty VHS copy of that Tarantino flick." She shrugged. "Anyway, I thought you could use a pick-me-up."

"Guess I'll have to save my sulking for another night." Blue opened the door wider and Domino pushed past him.

She sauntered through the tiny room, examining it critically. "Yours is better than mine."

"Paid extra for the view," he said.

Before the window were two cozy chairs flanking a worn rounded table. Blue sat down and Domino joined him. She leaned her head out the window, gazing down at the party.

"What do you think they're celebrating?" she asked.

"Who knows. But I wish I had something to be that happy about."

Domino smacked the table. "Quit being so blue," she said, and grinned. She stuck both joints in her mouth, lit them, and handed one to Blue.

He pinched it and took a steep inhale. The smoke just entered his lungs when he violently hacked it out.

"I remember the first time I smoked weed," she snickered before a drag.

Blue recovered and continued. His body began to tingle, his mind to feel like a weight and a cloud all at once.

"First smoke I've had in months," he said.

"You quit smoking cigs?" she asked.

Blue, realizing she hadn't seen his recent pack of Scythe cigarettes on the nightstand, only shrugged.

"Well, not during the climb, I should say."

"I see." Domino blew a ring of smoke, shooting another puff right through the center. "I'm getting too good at this."

"I think we're too good at a lot of things."

"Cocky tonight, are we?" she replied with a tilt of her head.

Blue gazed into her heavy eyes. The effects of the joint gave her a vulnerable look. Her Mia Wallace bangs hung lazily across her forehead; she swept them away with a flick of her head. Blue didn't like to see her this way. His idea of Domino was much different from how she acted while high. He guessed the look brought out her desirability. He always knew she was just that: desirable. But he'd die before admitting it.

"What I meant," he explained, "was that if we weren't so damn good at our jobs, maybe we wouldn't have been recruited to go poking around the ice for some stranger."

"I knew you were having second thoughts," she replied.

"It hasn't crossed your mind?"

"Nope."

"Why not?"

"Because it's something different. And we're getting paid." She took another hit. "What are you so worried about?"

"I just...I don't know." He trailed off, losing his concentration briefly.

"You've been thinking about the accident again, haven't you?" she said rather quickly.

Blue gave her a sideways look. She knew not to talk about it, but she also knew she was the only one who had the right to bring it up.

"No," he said bitterly. "It has nothing to do with that."

"You sure?"

"I'm sure, Dom."

"You got to talk about it at some point, slick."

"Yeah, well, tonight's not the night." He took a steep inhale.

Domino sighed. "Well, maybe I want to talk about it."

"Why would you want to do that?"

"Look, Blue. I know it's been a few years, but I am not good at just pushing that memory away and forgetting about it for the rest of my life like you."

"You think that because I don't talk about it means that I just forgot about it?"

"It sure seems that way."

Blue gave her an intense look. "He was my best friend, Dom. I think about him every single day. Each time I strap myself into a harness, or clip into a rope, or even step foot on a mountain I think about him."

"Then why don't you say anything?" she said irritably.

"Because I can't." He could feel tears well up in his eyes. He turned away.

Domino reached across and rested her hand on his arm. "You can't keep hating yourself, Blue," she whispered softly. "If you keep that anger inside of you, it's only going to kill you slowly."

"Well, maybe I like it," he said rather childishly.

"No, you don't. I know you, and I can see it eating you up every day."

Blue snubbed the joint out on the wooden table. He gulped, hoping the tears would go away. He had never been emotional in front of Dom, and he didn't want to start now.

"I wish desperately that I could tell you what happened," he said after a moment of silence. "I want to, Dom. I just can't, not right now."

She squeezed his arm. "I understand, Blue. But you have to talk about it. Not tonight, but soon. I can't stand to see you so out of touch with reality anymore."

Blue was confused by what she meant, but instead he smiled weakly. "Just give me some more time."

Domino finished her joint, then flicked it out the window. She stood and yawned loudly. "We got an early ride tomorrow. Best we get some sleep, yeah?"

"Yeah," Blue said, gazing again at the moon.

Domino leaned down and kissed him on the head. "Sweet dreams, handsome man."

"You too, pretty lady."

As soon as he was alone, Blue immediately relit the remainder of the joint. She needed to know the truth, she *deserved* to know the truth. But not now.

Redding woke them both before sunrise. Blue was already packed and ready, but hadn't gotten much sleep; the conversation with Domino was still lingering in his mind. But when he saw her, she said nothing on the matter.

"All right kids," Redding said when they entered into the lobby, "you all ready?"

"Been ready, Red," said Domino.

"What are we waiting on?" asked Blue.

"Our plus-four," said Redding.

Blue started adjusting the straps on his backpack when he heard a heavy bag hit the ground next to him.

"Not known for punctuation in the Southern states, are we, Mr. Greene?" Redding remarked.

Blue and Domino spun around to see a very tired Alex Greene.

"Y'all leave Georgia outta this, goddammit," he croaked, pointing at Redding.

"Greene?" Domino said in disbelief.

"How the hell did you get roped into this?" said Blue.

Greene shrugged his shoulders. "Money."

"What about Tenzing and my clients?" Blue continued, his voice slightly raised. "What about *your* clients?"

Greene laughed. "Did y'all see the sum on that check? Y'all got one too, I reckon?"

Blue looked at Domino. "Unbelievable."

"I handed 'em off to the Sherpas," Greene explained. "I did it in a fever. Just told 'em I had a family emergency."

"You're a real piece of work, Greene," Domino said, shaking her head in disapproval.

Redding jumped in. "All right, you people can have your family reunion another time. Our ride is here."

A befouled white, two-door pickup truck was waiting to take them out of the town. From there, Redding explained, the truck would drive to an unmarked grass airfield near the border of China where a twin engine Cessna would fly them to Shanghai. And from Shanghai, the Governor had arranged a first class flight to Alaska.

"I ain't ever flown first class!" Greene exclaimed.

Domino scoffed. "What a farm boy thing to say. Aren't you like, what, 35?"

"Why pay extra, it ain't gonna get you there sooner," Greene retorted.

Redding sat in the passenger seat, leaving Blue, Greene and Domino to jump in the back. Greene leaned on the rear of the pullout door and stretched out his arms on either side. He motioned for Domino to sit next to him, but she chose the end closer to the cabin with Blue, answering Greene with a middle finger.

The Nepalese driver acknowledged them once through the rearview mirror, then shifted the truck into first gear and off down the dusty road.

For three hours they wove down potholed streets and skirted along sheer cliff faces with no guardrails. Colorful buses passed by, packed with people who scanned them nonchalantly. Rhesus monkeys screeched at them from deteriorated temple walls. *Nepal at its finest*, Blue thought, knowing he was going to miss this place.

Greene broke his concentration. "I never did say sorry. About the kid."

"Thanks," Blue said emotionlessly.

"He was..." He trailed off, trying to find the word. "Strong." He nodded to himself, pleased with the word.

"Good," Domino scoffed. "Very poetic."

"I appreciate the sentiment, Greene." Blue gave him a smile.

"We gotta stick together in this world," Greene said, beaming widely with his signature, toothy grin.

"Tell that to your clients," Domino slung back.

Greene glanced over at her. "Maybe y'all haven't noticed, but aren't y'all pullin' the same disappearin' act as me?"

"Yeah, but *we* didn't lie to anyone."

"What's the difference?"

"The difference," she explained sharply, "occurred when you told whoever that you had some family crisis."

Greene chuckled. "Hold your horses. Lemme just holler to everyone on the mountain that the next president of the United States' husband has gone AWOL."

"There's other ways to go about it."

"Reckon you just have it out for me," Greene replied confidently.

Domino turned to Blue, who just shrugged.

Greene continued. "Anyway, with all this newfound money, I doubt I'll be headin' back to Everest."

"Of course you won't be!" Domino shouted, throwing her hands up.

"Hey, I don't owe no one nuthin'."

"You owe Tenzing," Blue said. "And definitely Jevel."

"All right, all right," Greene sighed. "I'll give 'em a little sumthin' from my 'inheritance' money." He shook his head. "I just think y'all are being hypocrites."

"Big word for you," said Domino.

"Okay, listen here you skinny b—"

"Enough!" Blue shouted. "If I have to listen to you bicker this whole expedition, I am going to lose my shit." He glared from Domino to Greene. "How about you two act like adults for once and just be civil with each other?"

"Be civil?" she echoed. "With Greene?"

"Please, God, just for my sanity," Blue sighed.

Greene cleared his throat. "Bein' the Georgian gentleman I am, I think I can engender a truce with the lady." He stuck out his hand across the bed of the truck and looked at Domino jovially.

Domino stared at his hand. Blue scowled at her intensely, hoping she could feel it. Finally, she reached out and shook limply.

"Y'see?" Greene said, happily. "Reckon that wasn't so hard?"

"I need to wash my hand," said Domino, wiping it on her pants.

"Christ," Blue mumbled. He stared out across the landscape.

Redding banged on the window with his fist from the inside cabin. "We're fifteen minutes out!"

Greene leaned back, looked up at the sky, and began to hum a country song. Domino sighed harshly, defeated. Blue silently counted down the minutes until they reached the airfield.

The Cessna was already parked and waiting in the grassland. A man leaned against the plane, thumbs hooked on his belt. He looked at the oncoming truck through his thick aviators but moved none.

Greene pandiculated as Domino and Blue piled out. Redding thanked the driver with a thick, brown envelope Blue could only assume contained money. The driver again said nothing and drove off the way they came, leaving the five of them with the plane.

As Blue approached the aircraft, he was almost startled to recognize the pilot. It was the apathetic Mr. Broadway, who opened the door and motioned for them to pile in. Redding took the copilot seat, again leaving the other three to cram in the back.

A headset was attached to each chair. After strapping in, everyone put them on as Mr. Broadway began flipping switches in the cockpit.

"Can everyone hear me?" he asked through the receiver.

A choir of affirmatives. Mr. Broadway turned the engines on and the plane lurched forward.

The aircraft bounced roughly in the grass, and Blue wished the wheels wouldn't fly off. Mr. Broadway took his time, struggling to gain speed. After a few tense seconds, he finally pulled the throttle back and the plane glided into the air.

Greene hooted in victory. "I feel like a goat in a briar patch!"

Mr. Broadway kept his cool. He wove around a peak of a mountain and turned the plane east. "There's puke bags in the back," he announced through the headset.

"They'll be fine," Redding said for them.

Blue hoped they would be.

Six

They landed in Shanghai a few hours later. Blue had always seen stunning postcard photos of the city skyline, but the airport gave him no such view. His disappointment didn't last, for when Mr. Broadway landed the Cessna, Redding shuffled them toward a 747 boarding from the tarmac.

"Good luck," Mr. Broadway said as they left.

Redding gave him a thumbs-up but produced no envelope for him. Blue turned and gave him a quick wave. Mr. Broadway tilted his head up and Blue thought he might have seen him smile.

As they climbed the mobile stairwell to the jumbo jet, a flight attendant greeted them enthusiastically from the top.

"Welcome aboard *Patriot Airlines!*" she chirped with a thick British accent.

"Evenin', gorgeous," Greene said with a tip of his hat.

"Ignore him," Domino said crossly.

"Thank you," Blue replied.

The interior of the plane was surprisingly unclean; the furnishings run down. Blue figured it was an older model. It was also rather empty for its size. It sat maybe three hundred, but besides the four of them there were only a few characters, all dressed in suits, seated about the cabin.

Greene and Redding sat in the front row, and Blue and Domino took their seats across the aisle.

"Window seat," she claimed.

Blue slumped down in the aisle chair and sighed in relief. His back was killing him from the torturous truck ride. These were the kind of times he wished he drank.

"How long is this flight, anyway?" Domino asked Redding.

"Something like ten hours," he answered.

Greene whistled loudly.

Blue glanced at Redding. "What happens when we land?"

"We get a ride to the nearest port. Then a boat will take us the rest of the way."

"A boat?" Greene exclaimed. "There wasn't no deal about no boat!"

"How else do you expect us to get there?" Redding replied.

"Uh, the same way Dr. Stone did." Greene pointed at the aircraft they were sitting in.

"No," said Redding. "Too much attention."

Alex Greene seemed nervous, which amused Blue. Domino noticed as well and Blue could sense she was about to say something clever. He gave her a serious look, causing her to retreat to the window.

The captain came on the intercom and gave out the itinerary. No stops, just a straight shot to a place called Barrow. Blue realized that this was in the middle of nowhere, wondering what business the well-dressed people from Shanghai had.

The engines began to whine, and the aircraft jolted forward and slowly gained speed. Blue was relieved to be on a smooth runway instead of the choppy field. He could sense gravity pushing against him as the nose of the plane lifted into the night sky.

When they reached cruising altitude, the flight attendant went around taking drink orders. Greene got a whisky sour and Redding a scotch on the rocks. Blue and Domino stuck with water.

"Fixin' to be a long flight," Greene said across the aisle. "Y'all sure you wouldn't like sumthin' to soothe the nerves?"

"I think it's best we all try and get some sleep," Redding cut in. "This is probably the last downtime we'll have for a while."

Blue knew Redding was right. He reclined and closed his eyes. "Keep an eye out," he told Domino.

Domino, who hadn't taken her eyes from the window, responded with a grunt.

As Blue began to drift off, something nagged him. It was the way Mr. Broadway had looked at him as he had boarded. He almost seemed to be smirking at Blue. Why? Broadway obviously knew something he didn't, and that's what bothered him. Sleep overtook him before he could drum up an answer.

Blue jolted awake, gripping both armrests, ears reaching for a bygone sound. He realized quickly that the aircraft was not moving. He bolted up but spotted Redding leaning against the chair next to him.

"You're a heavy sleeper, Mr. Jennings," he said. "It's almost impressive."

Blue scanned the aircraft. He was unsettled but couldn't quite put his finger on it.

"Prone to nightmares?" Redding said.

Blue ignored him, standing up. "Where is everyone?"

"Waiting on you."

They exited down the portable staircase. The weather was gloomy, the sky a muddy gray. Blue shivered silently, wondering why he was so cold. His body felt worn, his energy spent from so many days on Everest. But he knew if the team saw him struggling, he'd lose some respect.

He also did not want to be outlasted by Greene.

Blue followed Redding, who limped more pronouncedly than before, to a black van on the runway. The door slid to Greene's goofy smile.

"Mornin', Princess," he drawled. "Seems you were rode hard and put away wet."

Blue overlooked him and ducked inside. Domino, every inch as tired as Blue, lounged in the back and rubbed the sleep from her eyes.

"It'll be a short ride to the port," Redding explained. "The rest of the team is waiting."

The windows were tinted on both sides. Blue knocked on the glass with his fist; it was the strongest he had ever seen.

"It's bulletproof," Greene whispered to him.

"Why?"

Greene shrugged. "Maybe the aliens."

"Aliens?"

Domino chimed in from the back. "Alaska has, like, the most alien sightings in the world. People are always seeing lights and shit up here."

Blue laughed. "That explains what happened to Dr. Stone."

The chauffeur sped through the streets, swerving around cars. Blue enjoyed the thrill. His adrenaline began to pump through his veins; energy gradually returned to his body.

The van suddenly slowed and turned into a harbor. Blue studied the sailboats bobbing by the dock and wondered if they would be traveling in one. He spotted an enormous ship at the end of the moorings; painted black and red, it stood out clearly among the other boats. He knew immediately this was their vessel.

"There she is," Redding said in confirmation.

"Good Lord," Greene remarked, "now that's a dingy."

Domino leaned over to get a better view. "It's huge," she said.

"She's an Icebreaker, first of her class," Redding clarified again. "A tough one, I'll tell you."

The van came to a stop and they piled out hastily to get a better look. The hull, especially near the bow, was heavily scratched—scars from an epic expedition.

Near the gangway to the ship, three men stood talking amongst themselves. Redding motioned with his head for them to follow him towards the group. Redding greeted one of them, a tall scowling man in a trilby hat, with a brief hug. They exchanged short pleasantries.

"I'm Doska, Captain of *Busefal*." The man spoke in a thick Slavic accent, and pointed a fat thumb towards the ship.

"The huh?" said Greene.

Doska disregarded him. "These are other team members." He started from the left. "Mr. Duncan." An older brown-skinned gentleman smiled and tilted his head. "Mr. Hayes." A pale, scrawny middle-aged man with wire-rimmed glasses gazed down at his feet, offering no introduction.

Blue, Domino, and Greene introduced themselves. Mr. Duncan shook their hands, but Mr. Hayes offered a lackluster wave.

"Right," Doska continued, "we push off in fifteen." He peered up at the darkening sky and mumbled to himself. Then he turned and walked up the gangway to the *Busefal*.

"Anyone catch the name of this vessel?" Greene said. "The beautiful?"

"It doesn't matter," Domino said. "C'mon Blue." She motioned for the ship, but Redding blocked them.

"Actually, Mr. Jennings, a word?" he asked.

"All right," Blue said.

Domino sighed. "I'll see you aboard," she said, Greene trailing her idly.

Redding led him to a condemned warehouse in the middle of the frozen marina. Broken glass and debris crunched underfoot as they approached. It all seemed too sketchy to him, and for a minute he was afraid Redding had brought him here to do something conclusive. But as they entered the building, the sight of several armed guards calmed his nerves.

Redding pointed to a metal staircase in the corner. "Up there," he commanded.

Blue hesitated for a moment, but did as directed.

His footsteps echoed across the room. The guards studied him closely, clenching their rifles. Blue averted his eyes and sped up the noisy, metallic steps. He knew who waited at the top, but it still surprised him.

Arms behind her back, Governor Heather Stone gazed down from a dais at the ship. Dressed in a voluminous, violet overcoat, she exuded the authority of a surgeon surveying an operation.

Blue stood behind her, unsure of what to do. He removed his cap and cleared his throat.

Governor Stone spun around instantly, and to his surprise, regarded him warmly.

"Mr. Jennings!" Her greyed violet hair bobbed around her ears. She stepped down from the dais and strode over to him. "This is a great pleasure." She shook his hand firmly.

"I'm sorry, Governor Stone," he said, trying to tame his hair. "I would have cleaned up a little better if I knew—"

"Nonsense! I'm the one who should apologize." She placed a wrinkled hand on Blue's back and led him to a table by the window. The Governor was much older in person than she appeared on TV, but moved with teenage verve.

He slowly sat, regarding a chair on the opposite end of the weathered tabletop. He figured the Governor would sit over there, but she grabbed another chair and dragged it over to his side, placing it directly in front of him. She dropped down and folded one leg over the other.

"I want to start by saying how grateful I am to have you here," she said, resting her hands on a knee. "I know it was short notice, but as you know, the clock is ticking."

"Of course," Blue replied. "I completely understand." The Governor's kindness caught him off guard.

"I know you're a busy man," she added, "and I hope the money will compensate."

Blue smiled. "It was more than enough, thank you."

She nodded and looked away. "All of this is just...terrible. And it happened so fast. One minute he was here and the next..." Her eyes grew misty and she quickly straightened up.

Blue leaned forward. "We are going to find him. I promise." His own words surprised him. But her vulnerability played on his sympathy.

"I'm just afraid you won't find him in one piece," she sighed. "I told him not to go out there. The primaries are coming up and I need him here. But there's no swaying that man. Once his mind is set on something he is going to get it done."

"If you don't mind," Blue asked, "what is he working on up there?"

The Governor smiled. "My husband is a scientist. He has been fascinated by this planet since...well, since we met." She played with her wedding ring. "He was an astronaut back then. He had just come back from an important mission in space. I was working for Congressman Folkes at the time. The Congressman had invited Jay, my husband, to dinner to talk about climate change. That's how we met." She beamed, her eyes searching for that memory. "He was bald," she laughed, "very bald—and still is. But he carried himself with matchless confidence. Needless to say, he's the one who inspired me to follow my dreams. I wouldn't be where I am without him."

Her voice fell. "Politics is just a game. I'm sure you were told how important it is for my career that we find him alive. But none of that matters to me. I just want him back."

Blue was moved. He had pictured Governor Stone as someone who meant business, which he was sure she was. But here before him was a normal human being—desperate, plaintive, and humble. For the first time, he felt compassion for this woman and her plight.

"We will do everything to find Dr. Stone," he assured. "You picked a good team, a resilient team. We will not let you down."

A tear rolled down her cheek and she swept it away with her sleeve. Then she stood, smoothing the wrinkles in her overcoat.

"I know you won't, Mr. Jennings."

Blue stood and tried to meet her gaze. "I just have one question," he said. "Why me?"

The Governor sniffled, but managed a smirk. "Besides being an accomplished outdoorsman?" She patted him on the shoulder. "Some secrets are better left kept."

Her puzzling response annoyed Blue, but he couldn't bring himself to show it.

"It's all right," she said. "We'll have some time to talk when all this is over."

A ship horn blew to life and startled them, shaking the shards of glass around their feet.

"It's time," she whispered. "Now go. Please bring Jay back to me."

Blue nodded once and backed away, holding the Governor's confident gaze. He could feel the trust in her eyes. Then he turned, retreating to the ship.

Seven

The seas were rough but the *Busefal* held true, crashing through the surf with ease. In the belly of the ship, Blue weathered the rollercoaster. He also found, the hard way, that anything not nailed to the floor became an instant hazard.

Perched on one of two bunks crammed in the windowless room, he sat nursing a recently bruised arm. Across from him was Domino, who casually munched on a

black and white cookie. She flung the crumbs from her lap
and stared at the bottom bunk beneath Blue with sinister
joy.

"How you doing down there, buddy?" she taunted.

Greene, lost in the throes of seasickness, languished
in a ball and clung to a grimy bucket. He whimpered with
every sway of the ship.

"Can I get you anything?" Domino mocked in a
motherly lilt. "Soup? Crackers? Some nice, buttery
lobster?"

Greene's eyes bulged, and his head sunk deeper into
the bucket.

"For Christ's sake, Dom," said Blue.

"I'm just trying to keep my mind off things," she
whined, leaning against the wall. "I feel like a goddamn
prisoner in this place."

Blue glanced around. "It's definitely playing on my
claustrophobia," he agreed.

"So what did the Governor say?" she asked.

Blue eyed her curiously.

"That was who you met, right?"

"You've got a keen sense of smell."

Domino beamed with triumph. "I gotta be honest,
I'm a little bit offended she didn't want to talk to me. I
mean, I am the only woman on this testosterone-filled
rescue excursion."

"She wouldn't tell me why she picked us."

"Must've been our good looks." Domino sipped
from her canteen. "So what did the politician have to say?"

Blue rubbed his sore arm. "She just wanted to thank
me."

Domino snickered. "That's it? That's all she had to
say?"

"That was it."

"She didn't offer you a knighthood?"

"Nope."

"A castle."

"Shut up, Dom."

"But seriously, slick." Her tone changed. "She had
nothing to say but thank you?" She studied his face.

Blue exhaled sharply. "Well, she did mention some things about Dr. Stone."

"Like what?"

"Like he was bald."

"And?"

He paused. "He used to be an astronaut."

Her eyebrows raised. "Smart man."

"It would seem."

"What else?"

Blue scoffed. "Jesus, I don't know. It was a very quick conversation. She really didn't say much."

Domino reflected. "How did she act?"

"Morale-wise?"

"Yeah."

He looked away. "She was pretty upset. I genuinely felt bad for her."

Domino took this in. "So, I guess you're not second guessing this anymore?"

"Like you said, a lot of money."

"Don't compare me to Greene," she grumbled. "I see what you're doing, and I don't like it."

Greene moaned piteously.

Blue glanced at the bed beneath Domino. "Where's Redding?"

"No idea," she said. The light flickered and she glanced at the ceiling. "You don't think the power is going to go out?" she asked anxiously.

"Bless your stone-cold heart," Greene groaned faintly. "Afraid of the dark?"

"Greene, I will toss you overboard."

Blue cursed and jumped from his bed, heading for the door.

"Where the hell are you going?" Domino called.

The corridors were hardly wide enough to pass through. With each step, Blue felt the hallway getting smaller and smaller. The toxic cocktail of claustrophobia and high-seas dizziness threw Blue into a panic.

The cook—Jeff, he thought his name was—rounded the corner and passed by, pinning Blue against the wall for a few uncomfortable seconds.

"Watch it, Jim Bridger," Jeff hissed. Then, from down the hallway: "Can't handle a little water?"

Blue closed his eyes and breathed evenly. He needed to find a bathroom and quick. Stumbling down the corridor, he burst through what he thought was the restroom. He found himself in a tall compartment stacked neatly with large wooden crates.

A pathway of sorts had been shaped through the maze of timber boxes. Blue traced with his eyes to the other side of the room. At the end, watching him, sat Redding.

"Mr. Jennings!" he hollered out.

Blue made his way down, using the crates as balance. Somewhere in the chambers, Red Skelton warbled from a handheld radio. He clenched his stomach tightly, desperate to avoid puking. Above him, a lamp swayed back and forth with the waves. Redding watched him in amusement.

"Mr. Jennings," he slurred. A bottle of liquor was wedged between his legs.

"Mr. Redding, are you all right?" Blue asked.

Redding laughed breathily. "I should be asking you that. Looks like you're about to die."

"I feel like it."

Redding pointed his chin at the crate across from him. Blue climbed up and sat down, resting his head against another lumber package.

"Here," said Redding, offering the bottle.

Blue goggled at it.

"It helps with the nausea," he said with a grin.

Snatching the bottle, Blue took a stiff swig. "It's good," he lied.

"It's not supposed to be good," Redding said, retrieving it. He took a sip and stared off at nothing in particular. "It's nights like these that take me back." He sipped again, staring at Blue. "Y'know, I can tell you're curious."

Blue was taken aback. "About what?"

"About what I went through. You know who I am. Not at first, but you caught on. I see it in the eyes—your eyes." He pointed to his face with a shaky finger. "The way people look at me, I can always tell they know." Another sip.

"I don't really *know* anything, Mr. Redding," said Blue. "All I was told was that you spent some time up here. Stranded."

"Stranded." Redding's eyes took on a lifeless glaze, seeming to bore through Blue. "There were twelve of us came up here. Most of us had never seen the Arctic. One guy had never seen snow before, you believe that?" He chuckled to himself. "We were in over our heads, you see? Our equipment was old and our captain—the captain! The man couldn't pilot through the ice if his life depended on it," he spat in disgust. "And it cost him. Cost *us*."

Suddenly, his attitude changed. He swelled with rage and his voice rose like a dragon. "That asshole drove us straight into the floes!" He smacked his fist into his hand. "Right into the ice! By the time we knew what happened, she was already taking on water. We abandoned her just north of Siberia. Stayed afloat on two lifeboats. But that's when the trouble really happened."

Blue's mind raced with intrigue. Yet he wasn't sure he wanted to hear the rest.

Redding continued. "The ice water ruined most of our gear. Lost most of our food, too. We rationed what we could, but it was hard. We were weak, amateurs. The strong stuck with the strong, and those who couldn't hack it were on their own. There was no comradery.

"We had no leader; the captain was a coward. Everyone knew it, even him." Redding sipped quickly, spilling liquor into his beard. "Three weeks we floated with the ice pack. Conflicts were at a boiling point by then. Just as we were about to break, someone spotted land in the distance.

"It was an island, a small one. Wrangel Island, we figured. A rocky, desolate place. But it gave some reprieve from the icecaps. They move randomly; it drives you mad."

Redding passed the liquor to Blue, who took another sip and asked, "What happened then?" He wiped his lips and returned the bottle.

"We immediately started looking for food. We were lucky; the island was full of birds and seals. We were even luckier I grabbed the rifle and some ammo from the wreck." He paused. "And for the first week, things went well. Morale was high; I had a laugh or two myself, why lie? But one night, we found we weren't the only predators on the island." Redding cleared his throat and stared at the ceiling. "Think it was our ninth night there. A scream woke us up. We ran out by the fire, and that's where we saw it."

Redding skewered Blue with haunted eyes. "It was the biggest polar bear I have ever seen. Must've weighed over three-thousand pounds, Mr. Jennings, I swear it. It had our man in its jaws. He looked like a *stick*. Then it *slammed* him down so hard I heard every bone snap at once. And then it stood up on its hind legs. Over ten feet high, Mr. Jennings. So high, it blended in the dark." He stopped and closed his eyes. "The roar. I still feel it in my body. I will *never* forget that sound." He breathed deeply. "It nearly knocked us off our feet when it came back down. It took us in, rearing up, ready to charge.

"That's when I remembered the rifle. It was leaning on a rock nearby, and I dove. The beast looked at me, right at me, Mr. Jennings. It was going to kill me." He grasped a phantom rifle. "The first shot hit the bear in the throat. It played it off like a bee sting, and started coming for me. I put another in the leg. Nothing. A third in the neck. Nothing. My fourth shot hit it in the mouth, and it still kept coming. I knew I had one last shot. I put it dead through the left eye. And dropped it."

Blue couldn't believe his ears. "You're telling me you were attacked by, then killed, a three-thousand pound, ten-foot polar bear?"

"That's right."

"Forgive me, Mr. Redding. I find that hard to believe."

"I know how it sounds," Redding said. "But I tell no lies."

"So what happened next?" Blue asked, fearing another outburst.

"Our crewmate needed a proper burial. But the ground was solid, so we couldn't dig. We couldn't waste energy, so we covered his body with rocks on the hill by camp. The bear we ate, bar the liver."

Redding knocked back the last of the liquor and flung it away. It smashed against a crate, scattering over the pathway. He then reached behind him and produced another bottle. He tugged the cork with his teeth and took a gulp.

"How long were you on the island?" Blue wondered aloud.

"33 more days," Redding replied. "That's how long it took the bear to spoil and the birds and seals to wise up. So we had to make a choice: stay or go. Wrangel was a death sentence, but of course the captain ordered we stay. He said someone would come looking sooner or later. The man thought he was still in charge." Redding smirked. "Thankfully, our problem solved itself."

"What do you mean?"

"One morning the captain took an unfortunate tumble down the hillside. He was dead before he hit the ground."

Blue eyed him prudently. "So he 'fell,' huh?"

Redding held the bottle out. Blue looked at it for a long time, but eventually accepted it.

"We put him next to the first man," he continued. "We left the same day."

Blue drank. "Then what?" he said, offering the drink back.

Redding snatched it. "Then we spent another week drifting with the ice. Four days in, we ran out of food. I thought we had problems before. But nothing is more dangerous than a human being who's hungry and scared and fighting to live.

"We lost two more on the boats. Nothing we could do but take their coats and toss the bodies. It wasn't until the third man died we began to think the unthinkable."

Redding took a long sip, then squeezed the bottle with his knees. "We…ate him. Tore him apart like animals. It was…" He trailed off, staring up at the ceiling.

Again, Blue couldn't believe his ears. "My God," he said, and his voice almost broke. "You *ate* him?"

Redding continued to drink, averting his eyes. "By the time we hit Siberia, there were seven of us left, most of us nothing but sticks. Skin on bone like Inuit drums. So weak. Somehow, we carved a cove in the ice and set up camp. For days, maybe even a week, we huddled together. Then we lost another man. Again, we had to make a choice—the choice to *survive*."

Blue shook his head. "I just don't know how you could bring yourself to do that. Eat another human being."

The corners of Redding's mouth began to curl upwards. "Believe me, Mr. Jennings, go a few weeks without food and there is *nothing* you won't swallow."

Blue shivered. "So how'd you get out?"

Redding searched his memory. "It wasn't until we lost another that I started thinking I was really going to die. With six of us, we had to make a new choice, and that was who was strong enough to go look for help."

"Who went?"

He jabbed a thumb at his chest. "Which is why I'm here today." He tossed the alcohol onto Blue's lap. "See, Siberia's not as empty as people think. There are people, very few, who live and work there. When I started the trek, my hopes were to hit some kind of outpost.

"But I was dying, Mr. Jennings. The cold was suffocating. And the ice…the ice stuck to every part of me. I was freezing to death. Every step took me deeper into hell. But I couldn't stop. I couldn't give up. I had come too far."

Blue took a sip and handed it over. "What kept you going, Mr. Redding?"

Redding suddenly brightened. "On what was probably my third day wandering in the snow, I collapsed. Toes on my left foot were so frozen I couldn't even bend them. I was ready to give up. Spent, Mr. Jennings. I waited for death in the snow and ice. But that's when I saw something.

"It was a butterfly, Mr. Jennings. Out in the heart of Siberia. It flapped through the flurries, immune to the cold. I couldn't stop watching it. The colors were so alive. I followed it on hands and knees.

"In my mind it was Noah's dove. It took my last ounce of strength, but I kept crawling. I'm not sure how long or how far but I just kept going. The last thing I remember before passing out was lamplight cutting the haze. Turned out it was a man who just happened to see me. I was saved."

With that, Redding stopped talking. The two men sat in silence, listening to the creaking ship and the crashing surf, passing the liquor back and forth.

Then he continued. "He left me with some natives. They were good people, nursed my wounds. The only problem was no one spoke English. I tried to communicate. I tried to tell them there were still five men out there, but it was no use. Eventually, a trader who spoke some broken whaler English came by the village. Somehow, this man knew of our ship and crew. There had been people looking for us who'd given up hope. What a surprise I was about to give the world.

"I convinced him to take me far into the country, to the nearest town with a landline. The journey took two days, but with my foot in the shape it was, the man was kind enough to put me in a sled and have dogs pull me. After what I had been through, I didn't mind at all.

"By now, it had been a week since I left my companions in the ice cove. I had no hope, but I wanted to believe they were alive. When I made contact with the States, I told them everything. I gave them a general area to search, but due to bad weather, planes and rescue boats couldn't search the area anytime soon.

"I couldn't wait. I rented dogs and two drivers to take me back. I had healed somewhat, but I still had a way to go—my foot especially. But I had to get to my team. I needed to know their fate. See for myself.

"We pounded through the ice for days until I finally spotted it. The ice cove. I approached it with caution; I tried to prepare myself for what was inside. But..." His eyes darted around the room searching for answers he already had. "They were frozen solid, stuck to the walls, the ground. Human ice cubes, Mr. Jennings. And some...some had missing arms and legs, fingers. From what I could tell, they made a last-ditch effort to live any way they could. Even if that meant eating *themselves*."

Redding took a deep breath. "Now, Mr. Jennings, that is a kind of desperation only the dead understand." He knocked back a long sip and closed his eyes.

Blue's mind was spinning. He couldn't imagine Redding's suffering. There were no words of comfort, no gentle gestures to lessen the pain. There was nothing of solace he could give this man, and they both knew it.

"What happened with the bodies?" Blue decided on.

"It took us a while, but we managed to pry my friends from the tomb. I stacked them on the sled, and we left. Soon after, I was in a hospital bed surrounded by people I couldn't look in the eyes." He pointed down. "They had to take half the foot, by the way. But that's just how it goes."

Blue leaned back. "Mr. Redding, I don't even know what to say. It's all just so..."

"Horrible," Redding finished. "The worst part was coming home and seeing the families of the men we..." Again he looked away. "I had to tell them *something*. Say they died with dignity. That was the hardest part."

"I'm sorry," Blue said. "Really, Mr. Redding, I am."

Redding nodded. "So now that you've heard the whole story, what do you see when you look at me? Do you see a survivor, a man doing all it took to escape a frozen hell? Or do you see a monster, a beast who flayed his friends?"

Blue answered quickly. "I see someone shouldering eleven deaths." He leaned forward. "How do you see yourself, Mr. Redding?"

Redding laughed. "I'm just a man trying to make a living," he said, and knocked the bottle back.

Eight

By morning the weather had subsided. Clear skies and crisp air greeted Blue when he walked out onto the deck of the *Busefal*.

The drunken conversation he had with Redding had left him implacably unsettled. He could never comprehend what that man had gone through. He also wasn't sure why in God's name he would want to see this unforgiving no man's land again.

Reaching into his jacket, he pulled out a cigarette. He stared out at the infinite cobalt seas, at the ice caps around the ship.

"Reckon this ain't Kansas no more," said a voice behind him.

Blue turned to see Alex Greene, shielding his eyes from the sun. He walked over and leaned against the railing.

"How are you feeling?" Blue asked.

"Off like a herd of turtles," he said. He eyed Blue's cigarette with interest. "May I?"

Blue handed the Scythe over. "Dom still asleep?"

Greene inhaled, then laughed out the smoke. "Can't even sneeze in her direction without her tannin' my hide. Didn't so much as peep at her bunk this mornin'."

"True," Blue replied. "But it's your own fault for trying to make a move on her last year at base camp."

"Hah! She was spoonin' me, what was I gonna do?" Greene took another hit and handed the cigarette back. "She is a gorgeous woman, and it is my Southern duty to remind her."

Blue chuckled. "They do things a little differently where she comes from."

"No shit." Greene studied the water around them. "I'm fixin' to speak freely."

"Go for it."

"Reckon we're really gonna find, Dr. Stone? Alive, be it."

Blue pondered. "I'm not sure. Honestly, I'm not really thinking about that."

"Then what are you thinkin' about?"

Blue took a drag, trying to craft his words.

"Reckon it's the money?" Greene asked.

"No, I'm not thinking about that either."

"Well, let's hear it."

Blue tapped off the ash from the end of the cigarette. "Something isn't right here. I can feel it."

Greene nodded in agreement. "You're damn right. My mind's been runnin' all over hell's half acre and the math ain't addin' up."

"The math?"

"You get what I mean."

Blue continued, "It makes no sense that Dr. Stone would leave his wife at the biggest moment of her career to come out here for 'science' or whatever."

"Well, Redding says he *is* a scientist," Greene replied.

"Yes, but what's the rush? He packed up and came out here knowing full well the primaries are just around the corner. It just has me wondering what is so goddamn important."

"All right, let's draw on this," Greene said, folding his hands together. "What'd he do before he became a researcher of the ice?"

"He was an astronaut," Blue answered. "Went to space at least once, or that's what the Governor told me."

"So you did mingle with her!" Greene hollered.

Blue shook his head, ignoring the outburst. "An astronaut-turned-scientist, spending the rest of his days out here." He sighed.

Greene twirled his finger. "Maybe the man wants to help keep the world a'spinning. It's a noble duty."

"Maybe." Blue hit the smoke and passed it back. "I just have a strange feeling there's something bigger going on."

"Why hire us then?"

"I don't know."

"I got a mind to think Mr. Redding knows more about what's goin' down than us." Green inhaled. "He's slicker'n owl shit, Blue."

"I spoke with him last night."

Greene's eyes widened. "About the expedition?"

"About his accident."

"What accident?"

Blue filled him in quickly about Redding's history, leaving out the gory specifics. When he was done, Greene whistled.

"Feller's got some balls; I'll give 'im that," Greene replied. "You talk with Duncan? Hayes?"

"Not yet. I actually haven't seen them since we boarded."

"Reckon they know sumthin'?"

"Maybe."

Greene took one last hit of the smoke then flicked it overboard. "Did anyone mention how far we're fixin' to go?"

"Nope."

"Huh." Greene stood up straight, trying to balance himself on the deck. "My eyeballs are floatin'. I'm gonna find the commode," he announced. "And also my sea legs." He patted Blue on the back then walked off.

Blue bit his lip and considered his options. Then something occurred to him.

"Doska," he said aloud, then headed for the bridge.

The topmost room in the ship was sectioned into terminals housing a complex farrago of instrument panels. The computers formed a semicircle in front of thick plated windows that provided a panorama of the landscape. Most of the stations were littered with maps and diagrams of the area.

Blue found Doska bent over a nautical chart at the heart of the semicircle. Wielding a pencil and a bow compass divider, Doska slid his hand across the creased paper with surgical dexterity. Blue watched him with an impressed curiosity, unsure of whether to announce himself.

Doska spoke suddenly. "You look lost, Mr. Jennings."

"I actually came here to find you, Mr. Doska," Blue responded.

Doska continued to trace the paper. "You've found me."

Blue stepped closer. "I'm sorry to interrupt your work, Mr. Doska. I was just wondering if you could answer some questions."

"Moment, please," said Doska. He glanced at an open, leather-bound notebook on the terminal next to him, and started whispering numbers to himself.

Blue folded his arms behind his back, unsure of what else to do.

"Sit," Doska told him. "This is not military."

Blue took a seat in a skinny swivel chair.

Doska worked another few seconds before setting the tools down and turning to Blue. This was the first time he could clearly see Doska. He had a lazy left eye which appeared inutile. His skin was salty and wrinkled; Blue took him for a true man of the sea.

"So what is I can do?" Doska asked, chomping on a toothpick. He switched it between the corners of his mouth, studying Blue closely.

"I was wondering if you could enlighten me about a few things regarding the expedition," Blue asked respectfully.

"Shoot."

"Where exactly are we going?"

"Arctic," Doska answered, not jokingly.

"I...I know that. But *where?*"

"Research facility." Doska waited for a response, but Blue just stared back, unsatisfied. "Is hard to explain," Doska continued, grabbing the map and folding it out. "Here." He pointed to a dot along a bold line. "We are here." He ran his finger up the line and stopped in the middle of the water just shy of a land mass. "We are going here."

"To the middle of the Arctic Ocean?" Blue said.

"Technically island," Doska explained. "Was not before. Is now." He cleared his throat. "Does not exist, so is hard to find."

"I see," Blue replied, concealing his concern. "It doesn't exist for a reason, I'm assuming?"

Doska began to roll the map back up. "Probably you are right, but I could care less."

"So it doesn't concern you that we are sailing to this unknown place?"

Doska stared blankly. "Sail into void is why I am captain." He faced the window. "I name my ship *Busefal.* Do you know why?"

Blue did not.

"Alexander the Great had horse—Busefal. He was bolshaya—enormous…massive…and only Alexander could ride him. He rode Busefal in many battles; they say he could not die. He never once let general down. Every conqueror needs a partner. None better than Busefal."

"So you think you're Alexander, huh?" Blue chanced.

"Nyet," Doska said, spinning around. "But ship." He pointed outside to the randomly floating ice caps. "You can never win Mother Nature." He began to pat one of the consoles with care. "But with strength and guide, you can make damn good fight."

"No offense, but I am surprised you have such historical knowledge," said Blue.

"I like metaphor, Mr. Jennings," Doska responded. "*Busefal* has braved many battles, and I am proud to be Captain."

"Well I know Mr. Greene will be happy to hear about the mystery behind the ship's name," Blue joked, but Doska did not laugh. "Have you gotten a chance to talk with anyone on the team?" Blue continued.

"Nyet," Doska said flatly. "I have been busy."

"Are you aware of who any of us are?"

"I know Redding."

"So you know of his story? Of his time up here?"

"Da," he said. "I saved him."

Blue gaped. "*You* were the one who saved Redding?"

Doska allowed himself a half-smile. "I will never forget, I can tell you. I was not meant to be there." He shrugged. "Right place right time."

"Has he told you—"

56

Doska held up his hand. "Some things better not said."

"Well, I hope you know he was grateful."

Doska scoffed. "He told you?"

"He doesn't have to."

Doska leaned forward on the console, stopping just a few inches from Blue. "Let me say, Mr. Jennings. You survive that, you not grateful. If anything, I prolong his suffering."

Blue furrowed his brow. "You saved his life."

Doska shook his head. "Mr. Redding died in Sibir. Not physical. Mental." He slapped his chest. "Heart. There is no come back."

"You don't know that."

"Oh no?"

Blue stared Doska down. "Redding isn't the only one on this ship to come back from an ordeal like that."

Doska pulled back and studied Blue, gnawing on the toothpick. "So you eat your friends, da?"

Blue snorted. "Christ, no. But I know what it's like to watch them die. And I know what it's like to live on with guilt, wondering every second of every day why them, not me."

"You don't compare to Redding," Doska replied. "Yours was different."

"You don't know that," Blue said again.

"I not ask."

Blue glared at Doska for a moment, then looked down.

"We've all had Redding episode," Doska continued. "But his is worst. And sit and talk does not help."

Blue knew it was true. He had never wanted to speak about the incident with anyone, but after Domino brought it up in Nepal and last night with Redding, he yearned to unburden himself.

"As I say, some things better not said." Doska looked at him sympathetically. "It seems to me, Mr. Jennings, you have secrets too."

Doska saw right through him. Blue felt his skin crawling, but still managed a calm expression.

"Again, not my business." Doska turned to the window. "Now, excuse—I've got to plot approach."

Blue stood from the swivel chair. "Thank you for your time, Mr. Doska."

Doska grunted out an incoherent response.

As Blue headed for the door, Doska called to him. "Team meet tonight, 1900 on deck."

"I thought this wasn't the military?"

"My ship, my rules."

Blue didn't feel like arguing. "I'll spread the word," he replied.

Nine

The clouds had returned and darkened the sky. A draft stung Blue's skin as the whole team stood out on the deck in the front of the *Busefal.*

"Who are we waiting on?" Domino asked.

"Doska," said Redding, staring into the void.

"I'm freezing my ass off out here," Domino chattered, squeezing her arms tightly around her chest.

"Got plenty of body warmth over here," Greene declared, spreading his arms out.

Domino opened her mouth probably to spew some choice insults, but Doska came on deck and quashed the imminent quarrel.

"Come," he ordered.

The explorers formed a tight circle around Doska, who pulled over a crate to sit on.

"Do you know each another?" he asked the group.

Everyone looked at one another, giving Doska the silent reply he did not want. He sighed harshly, his breath fogging the air among them. "Go around," he said pointing to Greene first. "Say what do you do."

Greene flashed a polished grin. "I'm Alex Greene, winter enthusiast." He looked from face to face, waiting for a laugh that never came. "All right," he continued, "I guess my duty is to find Dr. Stone."

"Your job is help Duncan navigate."

"Right. Mr. Duncan. Navigation." He looked at the older gentleman across the circle and nodded.

Mr. Duncan chuckled. "Don't worry son, I've got no hard feelings towards the South." His voice was profound and stolid, but his expression was warm and welcoming. "I've also been studying the ice—pack movements and what not—for most of my days."

"Duncan is point man," Doska interjected. "He say keep move, keep move. He say stop, you stop."

"Just keep an eye on your feet," Duncan agreed.

Doska pointed to the scrawny man shivering silently in the wind. "Hayes."

Hayes removed his glasses with shaking hands, cleaning the lenses on his sweater. "I'm Tim Hayes, psychologist and medical professional," he muttered. "I've, uh, been working with trauma survivors most of my life." He shuffled awkwardly and glanced at everyone quickly. "I'll be handling any wounds we may encounter when we find Dr. Stone and his team." He put his glasses back on and looked at Doska for some sort of confirmation.

Doska just nodded. "You," he said to Domino.

"Okay," she started, steepling her hands together. "I'm Domino, and I guess I'll be taking care of this guy." She jabbed a thumb at Hayes, who avoided eye contact. "I've spent most of my life in the snow and ice, so I'm pretty much at home." She turned an eye towards Blue. "I'm also Blue's part-time caretaker, so play nice, boys."

Mr. Duncan was the only one to laugh.

"You help Hayes."

Domino squinted. "Of course! You would give the only woman on the team the 'nursing' duties."

Doska hardly reacted. "Problem, Ms. Domino?"

"I've got a problem with sexism. Just my opinion."

"You not paid for opinion," Doska shot back. "You're paid to work."

"I'd rather babysit Scarecrow over here," she replied, meaning Hayes.

Hayes looked indignant but kept his eyes down.

"Ms. Domino," Doska began, his voice slightly raised. "You no work, you stay with me." He gestured at Greene. "And he get your money."

This got to Domino. "Fine," she said. "But I'm not giving anyone any sponge baths."

"Fair enough. Mr. Jennings, now you." Doska smirked at Blue, but provided no hint of their earlier exchange.

Blue forced a smile. "I'm Blue Jennings, I'm just tagging along."

"You and Redding are communication," said Doska. He stood and kicked open the crate. Reaching inside, he produced a brick-sized satellite phone. "Vot." He said, handing it over.

Blue gawked at the behemoth. Its antenna resembled a pistol silencer.

Doska took the map and unrolled it over the box. He described the route he had explained to Blue, pulling out a pencil and circling the nameless island.

"What do we know about this place?" Duncan asked.

"What I know," Doska began, "is island is 1.6 kilometer. Barren, but many hills."

"Any idea where Dr. Stone's facility is?" Duncan questioned again.

"Nyet," Doska replied. "You go blind."

Duncan rubbed his chin, contemplating this.

Redding spoke next. "Anything else?"

"That's all." Doska retrieved the map, then folded his arms across his chest. "Questions?"

"What about food?" Greene asked. "Burnin' all these calories gives me a mind to eat the north end of a south-bound polecat."

"I'll bring some protein bars and snacks," Hayes answered.

"Protein bars," said Domino. "That's all we've been eating for weeks."

"One day tops," Doska assured them. "I call off at night."

"Call it off?" said Blue. "What do you mean?"

Doska looked down at him. "Small island, Mr. Jennings. No doctor? No team? All we can do."

"Y'all wouldn't leave us in the lurch, right?" Greene asked with a sprinkle of nervousness.

"You not back by dark, I blow horn. Two-hour warning."

"Two-hour warning for what?" Domino queried.

Doska frowned. "Get back to ship. Clock is tick. Stone is miss for week. He not here, he somewhere else. We not paid to look there."

Duncan eyed Doska cautiously. "What if we run into trouble? How will you know?"

Doska mimed a phone with his hand, pointing to Blue. "My number is program. I want updates by hour. You call no one other. Da?"

Blue nodded.

"Jesus, you sound like my ex-wife," said Greene.

"That be your cousin?" Domino smirked.

Greene looked at Blue. "You see what I gotta put up with?"

"Basta!" Doska yelled, putting a stop to it. "You professional, goddamn, act so."

Greene groused underbreath but the sound was carried away on the wind.

"More questing?" Doska asked again.

The wind howled.

"Dobra. If I'm correct, and I am, we arrive 0900. You leave ship, you follow Redding."

Redding bowed his head.

"Double-check tool," Doska reminded them. "Cargo has everything."

With that, Doska patted Redding on the shoulder and retreated to the bridge.

"He don't know dipshit from apple butter," Greene grumbled once out of earshot.

Duncan ignored him. "You all should get a good night's rest."

"There won't be room for error," Redding agreed. "We cannot afford to make mistakes. I don't want anyone playing hero and going off alone. Everyone stays in eyeshot."

"I'm not pissing while anyone's watching me, Red," said Domino, mainly at Greene.

"Treat this as you would an Everest expedition," Redding told the guides. "Same rules apply."

The wind picked up, sending tiny slivers of ice dancing across the deck. Hayes' teeth clacked loudly and Blue looked on with sympathy. Curiosity seized him—why would Hayes agree to this adventure? It was cold, Blue knew, but it was nothing compared to Everest.

Or so he thought.

One by one, the group disbanded until Blue and Domino remained on the deck. They propped themselves against the guardrail, smoking while watching the water lap against the verdigris hull of the *Busefal.*

"The ice is getting thicker," Domino noticed.

Blue had realized this as well. "Just means we're getting closer."

"Y'know, I'm gonna put this out there. I do not trust this Doska character." Domino watched the observatory with the corner of her eye. "He's shady, Blue. I don't like it."

"You never were one for trust," said Blue.

"I trust you, don't I?"

Blue inhaled. "We've come a long way since '89."

She smirked. "You were still calling me Cassi back then."

"Domino suits you better."

"It always has." She turned her whole body towards him. "Any regrets?"

"About what?"

"Anything, really."

Blue rolled his cigarette between two fingers. "Only when I think about the stuff I could have changed. On the mountain, specifically."

"That's what keeps me from wanting to go back." Domino chewed her fingernail. "Not sure I got another season in me, slick."

Blue was surprised. "What about all this push-through-it-macho-man attitude?"

"Everyone's got a threshold."

"Dom, you're one of the most talented climbers I've ever worked with."

She drew on her cigarette. "You flatter me."

"Seriously, Dom." He stubbed his own out and stuck the filtered end in his jacket pocket. "Where is this coming from? Are you really considering quitting?"

"Not quitting, slick. Retiring."

"And then what?"

"Something new."

Blue snorted. "Like go back home to your plush, comfy life, blowing through your family's money?"

"You don't get to say that," she growled. "You have no right. You don't know me."

"Oh, I don't?"

"That's right."

"I've known you for a decade now, Dom. We've climbed together. We've laughed together. Hell, we've even cried together." Blue paused as she looked away. "I've watched you barrel through impossible tasks, seen you pick yourself up countless times. What's changed?"

She sighed. "Honestly, Blue, it's because of you."

"What?"

"You heard me."

"Care to elaborate?"

Domino flicked her cigarette into the sea. "I look at you, the guilt you've been carrying around, and I think to myself, I sure as hell can't end up like him." She stopped herself. "I didn't mean it like that."

He shrugged. "Of course you did."

"What I meant to say, is that even I will break eventually." She took in a gelid gust. "Then I'll be stuck on that mountain forever."

Blue could still feel the jab of her previous statement. "Why is it that you're always going about saying I'm losing my mind?"

"I never said you were losing your mind."

"But that's what you keep driving at."

"I just want you to know what you're doing to yourself," she said with sudden intensity. "I *need* you to understand that what happened to Adam was not your fault."

The sound of his name spiked Blue's heartrate. This took him by surprise and anxiety took hold.

Domino picked up on his vulnerability and
continued to tease out the memory. "It was the storm that
killed him. He wasn't clipped onto a rope and wondered
off the side of the South Col, you said so yourself."

Blue gazed at the pulsating stars. Domino continued
to speak, but her words fell from his ears. He closed his
eyes, and then, just for a second, he was back on the
mountain. The storm howling across the Col; the frosted
tempest suffocating the air around him. He saw Adam
dangling along the side of a slope, his cries for help
drowned out by the gale. Blue looked at his hands; they
were gloved with a rope clutched tightly between them.
The rope then began to gradually slither through his
fingertips.

"He fell, Blue." Domino's soft tone brought him
back. "It's not your fault." She touched his shoulder.

"I just need some more time," he replied, shaking
her off.

Domino exhaled slowly. "He was my boyfriend,
Blue. I have the right to keep asking."

This was a thought that Blue wanted to forget the
most. Since Adam's death, Domino hadn't brought up the
fact that they had been lovers. He wasn't sure why it was
important now.

"You deserve to hear the story," he admitted. "But
not here."

"Right," she agreed. "But when this is all over, I'm
gonna hold you to it."

Blue wondered if he would be prepared by then.
"Fair enough," he replied. "But this retiring from Everest
idea—"

"Hold it," she said, sticking her palm out. "Let's not
change the subject here. One thing at a time."

"Just don't leave me in the dust."

Domino yawned noisily. "You know I'm not good
with goodbyes."

"That's what I'm worried about." He tried to meet
her gaze but she had already begun walking back inside.

"Get some rest, slick," she called back to him. "We
got another summit to mount."

Ten

"All right, let's go over the checklist." Redding was peering closely from his pocket-sized notebook to the packed bags in front of him "Mr. Jennings, you tracking?"

Blue had woken early to catch some peace and quiet before reaching the island. But Redding had the same agenda. They found themselves in the cargo hold, checking bags they had checked the night before.

"Canteens," Redding began.

"Check."

"Moon beams."

"What?"

"Flashlights."

"Oh. Check."

"Ropes."

"Uh-huh."

"Carabiners."

"Got it."

"Harnesses."

"Yup."

"Satellite phone."

"Yeah."

"Binoculars, compass."

"They're here."

They went down the list, accounting for more equipment and cold-weather-wear. When they finished, Redding put the notebook in his back pocket and slid into his bright red jacket. He had fastened a knife holster on the left breast pocket, the one Blue had seen him sharpen on Everest.

Blue assessed the knife closely. "Why're you bringing that?"

"Protection."

"From what?"

"Mr. Jennings, if you think I lied to you the other night about that bear, you obviously don't take me seriously."

"Forgive me for not believing in urban legends."

Redding chuckled. "Think what you like," he said, "but I know what I saw."

Blue contemplated his next words carefully. "Mr. Redding, I really appreciate you opening up to me last night. Really. I'm not minimizing what you went through...but a ten-foot bear?"

"I'm a lot of things, Mr. Jennings. I am not a liar. You'd be wise not to call me one." Redding tightened the straps securing his knife. "I was drunk. But honest. In vino veritas."

"I just don't think it's a good idea to go spreading something you may not have seen."

"So you're telling me I'm wrong to come prepared?"

Blue folded his arms. "We're looking for a missing man, not Bigfoot."

"You've ever been to the Arctic before?" Redding interrogated him.

"You know I haven't."

"How would you feel, Mr. Jennings, if I came to Everest and spoke out of my ass?"

Redding's barb took Blue aback. "I'm not telling you how to do your job," he explained. "I'm just thinking logically."

"We've got a long day ahead," said Redding. "Let's not kick-start it by pissing me off."

He was right. There was no need to argue. The peace needed to be kept and Blue recognized that it was on him to hold the team together.

"I'm sorry," Blue heard himself say. "My mind hasn't been in the right place lately."

"I can sympathize," Redding said. "Sorry to be so blunt. But it's the wild west out here, Mr. Jennings. The wild north. I need you to trust me."

"Okay," Blue said. "Can do."

They bumped fists.

Redding sneered through his thick beard. "Now all we gotta do is make sure Ms. Domino and Mr. Greene don't rip each other apart before we find Dr. Stone."

Blue started to reply but a most distressing sound cut him off. It started as a scraping noise on the hull of the ship. Then the *Busefal* began to shudder. The cargo wobbled precariously around them. Redding looked at Blue, but before he could speak, they were thrown to the ground.

Crates smashed around them, debris narrowly missing the two men. The contents, which appeared to be Egyptian artifacts, littered the ground. Redding sprang to his feet, grabbing Blue by the arm.

"You hurt?" he asked.

Blue was rattled but found himself uninjured. "What was that?"

Redding hushed him with a finger. "Listen," he whispered.

Blue listened closely. "I don't hear anything."

"Exactly. We're stopped."

"Did we hit land?"

"No," said Redding. "Ice."

Everyone converged on the deck. Blue assessed them quickly, but besides Hayes, who had a small cut above his left eye, everyone was fine.

Doska lumbered down the bridge and marched to port.

"Sukin sin!" he bellowed.

Redding joined him. "How bad?"

Doska spat in the ice. "Locked. Thought we could make. She always does."

Blue peered over the side. It was a foggy morning, the sky anemic and puffy. He looked down for flowing water, but all was frozen over. They had been subdued by the infinite ice pack.

"How close are we?" Duncan asked.

"Not far," he answered, watching the fog.

Domino spotted it first. "There!" she said, pointing through the haze.

Blue squinted into the mist. It had cleared just enough for them to spot a landmass with rolling black hills.

Redding rushed to the bow. "There it is."

"How in the Sam Hill you know that?" said Greene.

"That's it. It's gotta be."

Doska removed a golden spyglass from his back pocket, swiftly extending it. Putting it up to his good eye, he studied the island.

"Da," he whispered. "Eta ostrov." Behold the island.

"So how do we get there?" said Domino.

Doska called Duncan to port. "Duncan, walk from here?"

Duncan stroked his chin. "With summer starting soon, I'm not sure."

Redding interjected. "I don't think we've got a choice."

Doska paid him no mind.

"It's worth a shot," Duncan finally said.

Doska faced the group. "Nu. Stand up. Is time."

It was a long drop from the *Busefal* to the ice. Blue and Redding agreed that the best way to descend was by rope. With everything prepared, Redding ordered everyone into harnesses; Blue would stay onboard to belay the team down. Redding went first, swinging with ease. When he touched down, he stomped around the perimeter, testing the stability.

He gave a thumbs up. "We're in business!"

Duncan went next. Then Hayes, Greene, and finally Domino. She made no acknowledgement of Blue. This troubled him immensely, but now was not the time to concern himself with it.

When the team was safely on the ice, Blue handed the rope to Doska. He began to step down, but Doska stopped him.

"Tick starts now, Mr. Jennings," Doska reminded him. "Find Dr. Stone. Alive."

Blue heard a wisp of anxiety in his voice. Doska's face never changed but his uneven eyes flashed with uncertainty.

"We'll be back soon," he said, and jumped from the side.

At first, no one talked. They marched vigilantly in pairs—Duncan and Greene up front, Domino and Hayes in the middle, and Blue and Redding at the back.

"Check COMs," Redding called to Blue.

Blue reached into his rucksack and pulled out the satellite phone. He dialed the number programmed in and waited.

Doska's voice crackled through. "Mr. Jennings?"

"Can you hear me?" Blue replied.

"Loud. Clear."

"Good. We'll be in touch once we reach the island." Blue hung up and stashed the phone away.

The fog was thinning but still difficult to navigate. Blue surveyed Duncan carefully; he had a compass in one hand and orange flags in the other. Every few minutes or so, Duncan pointed down at the ice and handed Greene a flag to hammer in.

"Trail markers," Redding said. "Good call."

Duncan threw his fist into the air, halting the column suddenly.

"Unstable ice!" he hollered.

Greene pounded in a flag as Duncan paced ahead. As they waited for him to find a safe passage, Blue overheard Domino chatting with Hayes.

"So Scarecrow, how'd you get roped into this?"

Hayes shivered violently as a fierce wind pierced the convoy. "I used to work with Dr. Stone."

"When?"

Hayes coughed into his sleeve. "Mid-'80s. Before I got involved with TBI, I used to study the psychological effects of deep space on astronauts returning from long terms in orbit."

"TBI?"

"Traumatic brain injury."

"Was Dr. Stone someone you 'studied'?"

"Yes, he was one of the first people I saw when I started at NASA."

Domino whistled. "So you're a big shot?"

"I *was* a big shot," said Hayes.

"I see. What happened?"

He gave a small quivering laugh. "I was in an accident."

"Oh yeah?" she put a hand on her hip, poising for a retort. "Tell me more."

"It was a car accident."

"Oh." She lowered her arm. "So that's where this whole TBI thing came into play?"

"Yes," he said, looking away.

"So does it hurt?"

"Does what hurt?"

She pointed to her head. "Your brain."

"Mine? Oh, no," he stared at his feet. "It was actually my daughter."

Domino bit her lip. "From the crash?"

For the first time, Hayes looked at her. "Yes."

She lowered her voice. "Is she still..."

"Physically, she's alive. Mentally..." he shook his head, but continued. "The treatment was expensive. My wife and I could not afford to keep up with all the medical bills. I was going to have to quit my job and take care of her full time.

"Things were about to fall apart until Dr. Stone heard what was going on. I had only met the man a handful of times, so I was astounded when he showed up at the hospital. I was even more surprised when he offered to pay for the rest of the treatment."

Blue, who had been eavesdropping all this time, observed a rare compassion in Domino.

Her eyes darted away. "Dr. Stone paid all your bills?"

"The medical ones," Hayes smiled. "He took care of me. It's something I will never forget."

"That's incredible."

"So naturally, I never second-guessed myself when I told Governor Stone I'd help."

"You've got some stones, Hayes," she awarded. "Seriously, dude. And the whole deal about your daughter..."

"Thanks," Hayes replied simply.

Blue tuned out the rest, deciding instead to peer through the binoculars. He scanned the beachhead of their destination and reviewed the blackened sands. The hills, he figured, they could scale with ropes—this was the good news. The bad news: he couldn't see anything resembling a compound.

And then he saw something odd. A white mass jumping hill to hill. *Just clouds*, he figured, but he knew it couldn't be.

Duncan's voice came from their left.

"Over here!" he shouted, waving his arms. "I found a safer route!"

Blue let the binoculars swing. Redding glimpsed him from the corner of his eye.

"You ready?" he asked, his eyes narrowing.

For the first time in years, Blue knew he wasn't.

Eleven

They had been on the ice a little over twenty minutes before reaching the frozen island shores. The pebbles they traversed were slippery, so everyone stepped with caution. Blue looked at the rocks, the black sand, and wondered if he had stepped on another planet.

"What's the plan?" Domino asked no one in particular.

Redding studied the hilltops. "Move inland. But first, let's gather our bearings." He turned to Blue. "Mr. Jennings, you up for a little climb?"

"Always," he replied.

Blue had brought about a dozen ice anchors. He took them out, stepping back into the harness. Greene would be the one belaying him. Blue could sense his teeming excitement as they approached the hill.

"I can't recall if I've ever held the rope for you," he mused. "I also can't say I know of any fellers who climbed in the Arctic!"

Blue agreed. He *was* the only one of them to do what he was about to do.

"Don't fall," Greene encouraged.

"Thanks, Greene."

As he turned to ascend, he was surprised to hear Hayes' voice behind him.

"You whuh?" Greene repeated.

"I want to go up," Hayes repeated. "With Mr. Jennings."

Greene glanced at Blue, then back to Hayes. "Well, all right," he drawled. "But you climb up the exact way he goes. Got it?"

Hayes understood.

Blue cracked his knuckles and studied the hill. It was not a hard climb, and not too high, forty feet at most. He hammered in the first anchor and began to scale.

As he made his way up, he heard Greene giving Hayes much-needed advice.

"Hayes, you gotta nice ass, but don't stick it out so much. Keep that body close to them rocks. There ya go, use them legs."

Blue had never seen Greene teach anyone how to climb. His encouraging behavior took Blue aback. He had always figured Greene for a money-monger, but the sight of him guiding a novice made him consider Greene in a new light.

It took Blue ten minutes to secure a safe route. He hoisted himself up the final ledge and hammered the last anchor into place on the summit. There was little room to maneuver around the top, but the vantage point provided him with a good view of the environs.

From the perch, Blue spotted man-made structures below. Snuggled at the center of what seemed to be a meteor crater, a bunker-style building with an airplane hangar appeared before him. He immediately knew this was Stone's camp.

The sound of Hayes struggling up the final ledge broke his focus. He turned around and knelt, offering Hayes a hand.

Hayes obliged, and Blue pulled him up. Then he pointed to his recent finding.

"That's his camp, right?" Hayes asked, knowing there was only one way to find out.

Blue beckoned the team. As they ascended, Hayes asked Blue for the binoculars. Blue handed them over and basked in the natural beauty.

"It's a little spooky," Hayes declared. "It just looks abandoned."

"Can you see a plane?" Blue asked.

"Not sure, the hangar door is closed."

Blue waited, hoping Hayes would spot something worthwhile. But he reported no signs of life.

As they waited for the team, Hayes began to chuckle.

"What's so funny?" Blue asked.

"You ever hear the holes-in-the-poles theory?"

"No."

"In the early 1800's there was a man who claimed there were two giant holes—one in the North Pole, one in the South. He said these gaps were connected, that you could actually travel from one to the other. This guy was so sure, an expedition was sent out to find these openings."

"I'm sure they were disappointed," Blue replied.

Hayes shrugged. "They all died, so I guess we'll never know." He returned the binoculars. "I just hope we're not on a goose chase ourselves."

It was nice to hear this, because Blue had been concerned about this as well.

"I hope Dr. Stone is here," said Hayes. "I'm not sure I've got it in me to look elsewhere."

Redding suddenly rose on the summit and asked for the binoculars. He glared fiercely through the scopes down the crater.

"That's it," he said. "That is definitely it."

"It looks deserted," Hayes said.

"Maybe. Let's go see if anyone's home."

The hill evened out on the inside of the crater, so the descent was possible without ropes. The ground was layered with fresh, soft, ankle-deep snow.

Forming back into groups, the team slogged to the camp. The all-too-familiar treadmill feeling came back to Blue. It happened on Everest all the time: he saw his destination, and it felt so close, but no matter how far he trudged, he never seemed to get any closer.

It took a while, but they finally reached the compound. Duncan stood between the hangar and the concrete dugout, deciding what to check first.

Redding gathered everyone around and dispensed directives. "Duncan, Hayes, and Domino, go check the bunker. The rest of you come with me to the hangar."

"Do you think there's a secret knock?" Domino joked.

"Just don't break anything," Redding warned.

The team split up and went to their objectives. Greene caught up with Blue, bringing up Hayes' ascent.

"I taught 'im well," Greene complimented himself. "Reckon I can get 'im to come to Everest with me?"

"I thought you planned on doing something else?" Blue said from the corner of his mouth.

"Winds change," Greene retorted. "Sides, them's my stompin' grounds."

Upon reaching the hangar door, Redding made a startling discovery. Reaching into the snow, he pulled out a bulky silver lock and held it up in the pallid sunlight.

Greene scanned the garage-type door and found three latches, all missing locks.

"Reckon Dr. Stone ain't worried about looters out here," Greene figured.

Redding knelt and gauged the weight of the sliding door. "Mr. Greene, give me a hand."

Bending down, they managed to slip their fingers under the heavy door.

"On three," Redding said. "Mr. Jennings, when we get this open I want you to crawl inside. Got it?"

"Yeah." Blue dropped his pack into the snow.

"All right, ready, Mr. Greene?"

"More than."

"One. Two. Three!"

Redding and Greene grunted and strained. Blue didn't think they had the strength to pull it open, but the ice around the opening began to crack, and the door followed suit, but just slightly.

"Now, Mr. Jennings!" Redding howled.

In one swift motion, Blue dropped to his stomach and rolled inside. The door slammed behind him and blanketed all in black.

"What do you see?" Redding called.

"Nothing! It's too dark!"

"Use the moon beam!"

Blue replied that he left it in his backpack, outside in the snow.

"Use your smokin' powers!" Greene offered.

Blue had no idea what that meant. But then he realized Greene was referring to his lighter. He reached in his jacket pocket, removed the tool, and sparked it.

The flame stained the colorless room with a warm glow, and he got his answer immediately.

"It's empty!" he responded.

Redding's displeasure was muffled behind the doorway. "Well, see if you can find any clues!"

The fire flickered uneasily in Blue's hand. There wasn't much to see; the hangar lacked any furnishing. He was about to make his way to the exit when something on the wall caught his attention.

It was a white lab coat. When Blue pulled it off the hook, he saw a name stitched on the breast pocket.

"Stone," he read to himself. He folded the coat and returned to the heavy door, banging on it.

He heard Redding yell out another countdown, and the door cracked slightly open once more. Blue scurried out into the snow and handed over the coat.

Redding stared at it for a long time. "At least we know he was here." He squinted over to the bunker. "Let's go see if they're having better luck than us."

The flat, sharp-cornered roof of the concrete shelter was a bit of an eyesore, but Blue figured there weren't any neighbors to impress. There was a single window, or at least from what he could see. It was round like a porthole, with glass glossed over in frost.

The entry was more extravagant, the door painted black like the sands. It was very thick, and Blue wondered aloud how Duncan, Dom and Hayes got it open.

Redding found another lock lying in the powder, an answer to his question. He opened the iron door wider against the snow, and Blue and Greene crept inside.

Kerosene lanterns were hung on the stone walls. Blue felt something peculiar: it seemed colder in here than outside. He walked close to the lamps, hoping he could catch some warmth, but to no avail.

The bunker spilled into a cavernous chamber. In the dim room, Blue saw three metallic tables festooned with machinery. To him, they looked like car parts.

On the walls around them were maps of the area. Blue approached one and scanned it. They had been hand-drawn with impressive detail. He noticed red "X" marks randomly scratched in the parchment.

"Y'all reckon Dr. Stone hit oil?" Greene wondered.

"It would seem they found something out here," said Redding.

Domino burst in from a side door, rushing up to Blue and startling him all the further. She seemed shocked and her eyes darted about.

"Christ, Blue," she whispered.

"Dom, what's wrong?" He tried to match her gaze.

Duncan stuck his head out from the door. "You guys better come see this," he said.

Blue entered first and was smacked by a rank effluvium. He saw Hayes standing at a massive cage, caressing the iron bars. It was the biggest cage he had ever seen, seemingly made for an elephant. He noticed it was open when something caught his eye.

On the floor, surrounded by a carmine stain, was a severed arm.

"Holy shit," he declared, his skin beginning to creep. "That's an arm."

"A left arm by the looks of it," Redding observed.

Duncan bent down, shielding his nose and mouth. "Doesn't look too fresh," he said. "Few days by the looks of it."

Redding joined him on the ground and pointed to the stump. "Looks like it was ripped clean off. Like something very big and very strong pulled it right out of the socket."

"I would have to agree, Mr. Redding," Duncan gravely replied. "But what?"

Blue eyed the cage warily. Redding noticed; they understood each other.

"The floor beneath the cage is also a kind of elevator," Hayes said, fiddling with a lever on the wall. "But it doesn't seem to be operational."

Greene entered and recoiled. "Stench is bad enough to gag a maggot." He peeked at the limb with one eye. "Dr. Stone?"

"No," Duncan replied.

"How do you know?" said Redding.

Duncan pointed to the ring finger. "Stone's married, right? That finger should have a wedding band."

"'Less he took it off," Domino supposed.

"Either way," Duncan said, "it's a twenty-five percent chance."

Redding stood. "What else did you find?"

Duncan shook his head. "Nothing. The place is empty."

"No secret doors?"

"Besides the elevator?" Hayes called. "I think it's safe to say we've combed the place pretty well."

Redding rubbed his bald head. "This is quite the pickle," he said. "Not sure what to make of this."

"How about the plane?" said Duncan.

"Gone," said Blue. He revealed the lab coat. "We did find this, though."

Duncan scrutinized the coat. "This isn't going to be enough."

"So what do we do?" Domino asked Redding.

He turned to Blue. "Call Doska."

Blue pulled it out and picked the number. But for some reason, he couldn't get through.

"Must be the signal," Redding figured.

"I'll go outside."

"Good call. Take Ms. Domino and Mr. Hayes with you. I don't want anyone traipsing around alone."

The trio complied, heading back out. The wind was roiling, and Blue willed the storm away. From the center of the crater he couldn't see the clouds yet.

"Still nothing," he grumbled after the tenth or so attempt.

"Let me try," said Hayes.

Blue forked over the colossal object. "Go crazy."

Hayes received it and began to pace before them, stretching his hand towards the sky.

Domino sidled Blue. They watched Hayes stumble about for a minute in silence. Blue thought this was a good opportunity to bring up their conversation from the previous night.

"Hey, I just wanted to apologize. What I said last night—about your family's money. I was way out of line."

"Yeah you were," she said quickly. "But technically it's not my money. It's the government's."

"Still, it wasn't my place."

Domino cracked her neck. "Never told you how they died, did I?"

"No, but I've had my theories."

Domino bent down in the snow, grabbing a handful of ice. "I had just turned thirteen. Being an only child, my birthday was a big deal for my parents. I was definitely spoiled, as you know. I got everything I asked for." She carefully molded the ice into a ball. "Being the daughter of a US ambassador, we traveled a lot. Spent most of my childhood in Europe. It was in Africa though, when it happened."

Domino tossed the snowball into the air repeatedly. "We were traveling in a convoy of three SUVs when the rebels attacked. They ambushed us on three sides; blew the first car up with some kind of rocket, then hit us with machine guns. I remember lying in the back seat, my parents telling me everything was going to be all right." She shook her head, throwing the snowball off into the distance. "My dad knew they were coming for him. We didn't have much time before the rebels advanced on us. Most of the bodyguards had been killed, even our driver. My dad pulled his body into the backseat and told me to hide under him."

"Jesus, Dom," Blue said. "You were—"

"I had known that man for years. He had been shot in the face, and I couldn't recognize him. But I knew who it was. My dad covered me with his body. And then he smiled at me. Assured me, my mom, that he would work everything out. He stepped out of the car, and then I heard the shots. They cut him down before he could say a word. And my mom…" She kicked the snow hard. "They never found me, though. I laid there until they left. They were laughing, I remember. Like it was all a game." She spat. "Savages."

Blue turned from her. "I don't know what to say, Dom. I had no idea."

"Ain't your fault, slick. That's just how it goes, y'know?"

"How what goes? Life? What happened to you is not okay, and you know it."

She shrugged. "I've dealt with it. It's in the past now. If I let what I went through eat me up, then I never would have accomplished what I have today."

"I'm proud of you," Blue said. And then he thought of Adam. He wondered if he knew. "I see now why you're worried about me."

"I can't make you forget the past, slick. You shouldn't. But you can't let it kill you, I've told you before."

Blue began to feel incredibly selfish. Domino had been through a horrible experience and had never spoken a word about it until now. He wondered how this woman had coped for so long. He wondered how much time he had left to cope with his own demons.

"Listen," he began, "I've wanted to tell you about—"

"The hell?" she exclaimed.

"What?"

"Hayes! He's gone!"

Blue whipped forward, scanning the area. Hayes was nowhere to be found. Blue cursed loudly and ran through the snow, fervidly scouring the powder. As he fumbled, he spotted a swale in the ground and moved towards it. He stood just shy and looked down.

There in the snow was a round, colossal pit. Blue panted, peering into the crevasse.

It was the deepest hole Blue had ever seen. It tunneled straight down, disappearing into soupy blackness.

Blue cupped his hands and roared as loud as he could to Domino. "Get Redding!" his voice quivered in desperation. "Now!"

Twelve

Redding got there with remarkable speed, beating the rest of the team by a good margin. He had a rope in one hand and a flashlight in the other. When he reached the pit, he clicked the beam on.

"Goddamn." He shone the light down the dark. "There's no end."

Blue knelt. "Hayes!" he shouted. "Hayes! Can you hear me?"

Nothing. The wind skating over the ice was the only sound on the entire island.

The rest of the team arrived, gasping for air. Duncan, the old man, seemed the least tired. He dropped to his hands and knees, sticking his head over the abyss.

"Hayes!" he thundered.

Once again, nothing. Redding began to tie the rope around his waist, but Duncan stopped him.

"No," he said. "It's no use."

"No use!" Domino shouted. "He's down there, we have to try!"

Redding didn't fight it. He knew it too. He snapped the rope with a flick of his wrist, defeated.

Greene wheezed heavily from behind. "There's gotta be a way."

Duncan shook his head. "Who knows how deep this goes? There's no way he would survive."

"You don't know that," Domino argued. "He could just be knocked out; I've seen it before."

"We don't have the time or power to go looking for someone else," Redding pushed.

Greene bent down. "We should buzz Doska. Like, now."

Redding agreed. "Phone."

Blue chewed his lip and looked down. "Hayes had it," he murmured.

"What?" Redding snarled. "Why did Hayes have the COM?"

Blue knew it was pointless to defend himself, but he tried anyway. "He wanted to see if he could get a better signal," he admitted. "I never thought anything of it."

Redding scowled at him. "Well, I bet you're thinking about it now."

"Watch yourself, Red," Domino stepped in. "This is not his fault."

Redding ignored her and faced Duncan. "It's best we call it."

"I think you're right," he replied, deflated.

Greene squinted. "Call whuh?"

Redding positioned himself so everyone could see him. "Stone is not here and we've got another MIA." He needled Blue from the corner of his eye. "And no COMs. We should go back and weigh our options."

No one opposed him. They decided to retreat to the *Busefal.* Redding never waited for them to fall in line; it seemed to Blue that at this point all order was out the window.

As they marched back, Blue fell behind and hung his head in shame. Domino noticed and dropped back, draping an arm around his shoulder. She whispered in his ear that this wasn't his doing, but Blue did not listen. Hayes had literally disappeared before him and he could not make sense of it.

"Look at me," she demanded.

Blue could not. He bit his cheek and watched his feet crunch the snow.

"We're going home now, Blue," she said. "We'll get you some help, I promise."

"Don't pity me," he said harshly.

"I'm not, slick. I just care, you know that."

Blue pulled away. "I just want to get back," he grunted.

Still gazing at his feet, he ran into Greene and nearly knocked him down. He expected some kind of brawl, but

Greene said nothing. He continued to stare off in the distance, at the other side of the crater.

"Y'all see that?" he said. "Down yonder."

Redding turned around. "Whatcha got, Mr. Greene?"

"Ain't sure. Looks like some kinda pillar."

Redding pulled out the binoculars. He held them up, peering out intently.

"Well, shit." Redding lowered his arms and looked at everyone. "It's the plane."

The wreckage blended with the snow. If it didn't look so unnatural against the crags, it likely would have remained hidden forever. How Greene spotted it, Blue would never know.

They hurried to the crash site in total silence. Blue was soaked in dread, uneasy about the carnage ahead. But he pushed forward, faster than everyone, even Redding. He had to reach it first. He *needed* to be the first one there.

He stopped just shy of the Cessna. It lay on its side, half coated in snow, its left wing jutting up like an abstract sculpture.

Redding came second in the sprint. He wasted no time ogling it as Blue had. He climbed up the side and shuffled his way to the pullout cabin door.

"There's too much ice!" he yelled.

Greene had the pickaxe but was too far back. Redding groaned to himself, unsheathing his knife. He choked up on the handle, and began to chip away at the icy casing around the plane.

"Don't just stand there, Jennings!" Redding barked. "Help me!"

Blue snapped back to reality and began to plunder the debris for an object. He fished out a steel-plated section of wing and joined Redding by the access hatch.

Gripping the object with both hands, Blue hacked away at the ice, weakening it with some success.

Domino finally reached them, joining the struggle and hammering her flashlight on the sheet.

It took a few minutes, but they were finally able to punch an opening around the outside latch. Redding returned his knife, gasping from the effort.

"Mr. Jennings…up here," he managed.

Blue clambered up and wedged himself by the doorway between the fragmented wing and another snarl of wreckage. Redding crouched and squeezed the handle, pulling with all his strength. Repositioning himself, he tried again.

"This isn't working."

Blue had a thought. "Let's use the rope."

Redding grabbed his chest and uncoiled the rope sashed around his upper body. Looping it around the handle, he tightened it with a quick knot and tossed it to Blue.

Blue gripped the fibers firmly and heaved as hard as he could. "Is it working?"

"Not yet." Redding slid down and called for the rope. Blue tossed it down; Redding and Domino took over, straining indomitably.

A sound like a snapping tree erupted from the doorway, blasting Redding and Domino backwards. Redding recovered quickly and scrambled to his feet.

"Is he in there?" he demanded.

Blue steadied his breathing and tried to steel himself for what he was about to see. But he knew no amount of bracing could prepare someone for this.

Domino tossed up her flashlight. Blue stuck a leg inside and turned on the beam.

His voice quaked. "I've got bodies in here."

Just then, Duncan and Greene came up.

"What did he say?" Duncan wheezed.

"We found 'em," Redding said.

"Jesus." Greene turned away and covered his mouth.

Domino stood with arms akimbo. "All four?"

Blue forced himself to look again. It was a cataclysmic mess; equipment harum-scarum, wires snaking from the walls. The corpses were torqued into mangled yoga poses, staring out like subjects of an Edvard Munch painting.

Tossing what he could to clear more space, Blue
began to count.
"There's only three!" he called, but knew it couldn't be
right.
"Check again!" Redding ordered.
He did. Again, he concluded there were only three
men.
"Switch," Redding commanded, and climbed back
up. Blue relinquished the light. Redding dove inside.
"Any of them Stone?" Duncan said impatiently.
Redding searched noisily as they waited in silence.
Blue closed his eyes, trying to imagine the Governor getting
news about their failure.
"The son of a bitch is not here!" Redding bellowed.
"You sure?" Duncan asked.
"Stone's bald as a grape," he said, sticking his own
grapelike head out from the wreckage. "Unless he magically
grew a full head of hair, none of these guys are him."
"Anyone missing an arm?" Blue hazarded.
Redding nodded. "Guy in the back has his left arm
severed at the bicep."
Duncan wanted to see. Redding helped him up, and
he landed clumsily inside. Perching himself on the wing,
Redding dangled his feet and stared upwards.
"Where the hell could he be?" he wondered aloud.
Blue began to think, trying to keep his mind off what
he had just seen. "This is going to sound crazy," he began,
"but did it not take three of us to pull that door open? Is it
possible that he wasn't in the plane when they left?"
Redding stroked his beard. "So you're suggesting he
was never in the plane?"
"Is that too far-fetched?"
"Hold your horses," Greene interrupted, "why'd y'all
reckon they leave without 'im?"
"I bet it has something to do with that cage,"
Domino said.
Greene started to pace nervously in the snow.
"None of this is makin' a lick of sense. What the *hell* kinda
tree we barkin' up?"
"Calm yourself, Mr. Greene," Redding moaned.

"What's the plan?" Domino asked no one in particular.

Duncan dropped from the aircraft. "Retrace our steps."

Redding agreed. "We need to head back to Stone's camp and prod around." He watched the hills warily as the wind increased.

"What about Doska and the ship?" Domino added. "And Hayes? We could split up and—"

"Negative," Redding stopped her. "Let's not forget why we're here."

"So you're just going to change your mind?" Domino said, standing defensively. "We know why we're here. Why don't you show some respect for Hayes?"

"Respect!" Redding scoffed. "The man fell through the fucking earth. We're not going to find him. That's not respect, that's brains."

Domino turned to Blue. "You believe this guy?"

Blue opened his mouth but Duncan spoke up. "I know what you're trying to say, Dom," he said. "Mr. Redding may be brusque, but he has a point. Our mission is to find Dr. Stone. That's why we're getting paid." He paused. "What happened to Mr. Hayes is completely unfair. But we all knew the risks."

Blue avoided Domino's unrelenting stare, once again finding his feet a better sight. His body language revealed his alliance.

A rumble filled the air and a pack of clouds began to darken the sky. Snow started to flurry around the team, and in less than a minute the storm was upon them.

"Grab your gear—back to the bunker," Redding ordered.

"What about these bodies?" Greene pressed.

"They'll be safer in there," Redding pointed to the plane. "We'll mark it on the map, but right now we need to get moving, ASAP."

Blue saw the compound in the distance, and knew they needed to hurry.

Thirteen

Somehow, they arrived just as the weather worsened. Redding held the entryway open against the caterwauling wind, waiting for the group to pile in. He slammed it shut, barring it with a hefty metal latch.

The team was spent, especially Domino. She sprawled in a chair in the big room and leaned back, grimacing at nothing in particular. Greene claimed he was going to look for kindling and disappeared around the corner.

Finding no other chairs, Blue grabbed a seat on the cold ground across from Domino. Duncan relit the lanterns and joined him, along with Redding.

"Goddamn!" Redding groaned. He leaned on the wall, sliding down until he hit the concrete. Blue and Duncan watched as he untied his left boot, yanking it off painfully. When he removed his sock, Blue was surprised, even though he was told before, to see his foot halfway amputated. It had been cut past the ankle, but the rest of the foot was covered by a prosthesis.

"It's called a Syme's amputation," he said, feeling their eyes. "I'm lucky they didn't take the whole ankle."

"Does it hurt?" Blue wondered.

"Quite a bit," he replied. "But it's just a foot. I've still got my life."

"It's been hard, hasn't it?" said Duncan. "My father lost his leg on the beaches of Sicily in '43. I'm not saying I understand, but I empathize."

Blue pulled out his crushed pack of Scythes and lit one. He offered one to Duncan, who declined. Redding, however, chose to partake.

He took a smooth drag. "There goes ten years down the drain."

Blue sighed. "Damn, I didn't know that."

"You're a bad influence, Mr. Jennings," Redding joshed, dangling the cigarette from his mouth as he massaged the stump around the prosthetic.

Duncan changed the subject. "You guys think we're going to find him?"

"Who?" Redding asked.

"Dr. Stone."

"Oh. Alive?" Redding took a puff. "Probably not."

Blue shook his head. "I didn't expect things to turn out like this. I thought we'd come up here and find him looking in a microscope. Ice samples or something."

Duncan agreed. "I heard you spoke with the Governor before we pushed off."

"Yeah," Blue said. "She was upset. She loves this man; I could see it."

Duncan leaned back. "I see. Have any of you been married?"

Blue and Redding both shook their heads.

"Love is a funny thing," Duncan sadly stated.

"So I've heard," Redding replied. "Were you ever tied, Mr. Duncan?"

"I was once. But there was only one woman I ever loved."

"Not your wife?"

Duncan grinned. "As messed up as it sounds, I never much cared for her. She came into the picture way after everything went down."

"What was her name?" Blue asked.

"My wife's?"

"No, this woman you loved."

Duncan smiled wider than Blue had ever seen. "Her name was Serenity, and she was the sweetest soul to ever grace the earth. I mean it, guys. We didn't deserve her. She's the kind of gal you wanted to get caught staring at, just 'cause it meant she'd be acknowledging you in some way. I'll never forget the first time I saw her. It was at a bar." He began to chuckle to himself. "This sounds cliché, but when I looked in her eyes I could actually feel my heart instantly liquefy inside me." He stopped. "But in the good way."

Blue tilted his head. "So did you talk to her?"

Duncan broke eye contact. "Not at first, I don't know why. It might be hard to believe now, but I was once a dapper young glass of water."

Redding burst into tired laughter.

"I'm serious. I had no trouble with women. Honestly, I treated most of them pretty shitty because I never cared. I moved from gal to gal knowing there was always someone better. So trust me when I say...I tried with all my might *not* to go over there."

"What?" Blue exclaimed, enjoying the warmth of Duncan's story. "Why?"

"A woman who makes you feel that way with her eyes, she's already broken your heart. I knew if I met her, that would be it."

Redding leaned forward. "So you loved a woman you never talked to?"

"No, no, I eventually nutted up. I was lucky—it was the end of the night and the place was emptying out. I tried to woo her with fauxsisticated language and hardcore stories about coming out on top. She x-rayed my bullshit though. I must have done something right, because before she left, she gave me the blessing of her phone number."

Duncan continued. "I never expected her to call back. Women that beautiful always have a guy. But, again, I was blessed."

Blue coughed into his arm. "So did you guys date?"

"We went steady for a while." Duncan stared longingly off. "Never had so grand a time in my life. I was twenty-two, but I couldn't remember the last time I had so much fun with a gal, or anyone. When we weren't together, I felt incomplete. Couldn't think, couldn't eat, sleep. She was on my mind 25/8."

"Sounds horrible," Redding said, flinching from a sore nerve.

"Love is the best and worst thing for a man," Duncan explained. "When you care about someone as much as you, you do not want to lose it. But I was broken. I didn't know how to make it last. I got pissed when we couldn't hang and jealous when she talked to other fellas. She was so kind and gentle, and I didn't want to let that go.

"I spouted off one night, said some stupid shit. Stuff I couldn't take back. I said it 'cause I was scared of feeling this way. My mind was telling me two different things and I couldn't handle it. She ended up moving away and I never got to say goodbye."

Blue saw the tears spring in Duncan's eyes. Redding noticed it too, and looked away.

Duncan wiped his nose. "It's my biggest regret. I had the perfect woman and I lost her to my temper. I was so sad for so long; I just didn't give myself time to get used to happiness. If that makes sense."

Blue snubbed his smoke. "You never saw her again?"

Duncan shook his head. "This was over thirty years back, and it still hurts like yesterday. If I could go and change one thing, I'd deck myself in the teeth."

"If you had that chance, why wouldn't you just go back and stop yourself from talking to her at all?" Redding said sourly.

"She gave me a reason to live." Duncan held him with wide eyes. "She gave me confidence I never thought I could have. She broke my heart, which was all *my* fault, but I still keep those memories. I didn't want to let her down. I thought maybe if I turned my life around, I could get her back."

"But you didn't," Redding said.

Duncan shook his head. "There's just some things you can't come back from. I could have changed, but I hated myself. And I never had the cojones to ask for help." The old man fiddled with a stray thread on his jacket. "We can't fix the past no matter how hard we try. We just have to try not to repeat mistakes."

Redding finished his massage, carefully harnessing the prosthetic on. "So what does this have to do with Dr. Stone?"

"It's got nothing to do with Stone." Duncan pointed to them. "This has to do with the both of you. Take it from an old man, life is too short to hate yourself. I've only spent a few days with you two, but I see it in your face, the hate you hold inside. Gotta let that shit go."

Redding knotted his boots and stood with a grimace. "Thanks for the peptalk, Mr. Duncan. But like you said, you can't change the past." He left the room, leaving Blue and Duncan alone.

Blue leaned in. "How do you know?"

"How do I know what, Mr. Jennings?"

"How can you tell I hate myself?"

Duncan pointed to his eyes just as Redding had. "I see it in here. The eyes say what the heart is thinking. And your heart is dealing with something deep."

Blue turned away and found himself gazing at Domino.

"I see the way you look at her," Duncan noticed. "I see the way she looks back."

"It's complicated," Blue replied.

"Always is."

"But really," he said, turning back to Duncan. "I did something horrible too. She doesn't even know."

"Couldn't have been worse than me."

"No," Blue asserted. "It is."

Duncan processed his statement carefully. "And you can't tell her?"

"I can never tell her."

Duncan put a hand on his shoulder. "You gotta let it go, Blue. No matter how hard it is. If you can't be honest with her, you'll lose everything."

Blue knew he was right. But before he could reply, Greene shot into the room.

"Hey." He seemed more hesitant than usual. "I found sumthin'. Y'all best come check this out."

Domino opened her eyes. "It better be that kindling."

"No," he riposted. "Y'all come with me."

Greene was referring to a secret passageway they had overlooked. He led them to a wall in the same room as the giant cage, and pointed.

"The wall's open," he said. "Y'all remember that?"

"Guess we didn't see it," Redding muttered, nearing the concrete wall.

Blue ambled over, gaping at the thickness of the proscenium. "I feel like we're about to enter an Egyptian crypt," he remarked.

Redding snapped his fingers. "Moon beams."

Blue removed his flashlight and waited on Redding, who peered carefully into the doorway.

"Reckon Stone's in there?" Greene asked quietly.

Redding peeked back to the group. "There's a staircase, but it's narrow. I think I'll go it alone."

"No way," Blue found himself saying. "If he's down there, I don't want to be all the way up here when you find him."

"Same," Domino said, stepping forward. "I'm going, too."

Redding didn't argue. He looked at Duncan and Greene. "What about you two?"

"I was never good with stairs," Duncan replied. "I think I'm going to sit this one out."

Greene chimed in. "I think that Everest expedition is finally catchin' up on me. I'm fixin' to stay on the sidelines as well."

"Reckon so," Domino mocked with a Southern accent.

"All right," Redding said, opening the door wider. "Stay close."

Fourteen

The stairwell was much narrower and darker than Blue had expected. It curved steeply to the left, only allowing one person to move down at a time.

Domino rubbed her hand against the rock wall. "I feel like we're going into a dungeon."

Blue felt the wall as well. "Or Hell."

They descended nearly ten stories before the staircase opened into a corridor. They were greeted by a red strobe light that flashed above a wire-framed fence in their path.

Redding approached the gate and tried to push it open. "Locked."

Blue watched closely as he palpated the links. Redding's hands moved with swift fluidity, familiar with this type of contraption. Seconds later, he shined the light near the gate handle.

"Look here," he said. "Some kind of card scanner."

Blue and Domino drew in to get a better look.

"Don't suppose they have a spare lying around," she sighed.

Blue yanked at the fencing, but Redding said it was fruitless. "We need to find the key card. That's the only way we're going any further."

At the other end of the hallway, past the fence, was a bulkhead door that seemed to come from a Navy vessel. The red light cast it in an eerie glow, and it truly seemed they were entering Dante's Inferno.

Domino clicked her tongue. "Secret passages, giant cages, flashing lights..." She threw her hands on her hips. "What kind of facility was Stone running?"

"We can find out later." Redding walked back towards the stairs. "C'mon, let's tell the others."

When they ascended, the squall had gotten fiercer. The wind pounded the compound exterior. Even through the concrete, Blue could feel the gnashing of the cold.

"What did you find?" Duncan asked.

Redding told them about their findings and the missing key card.

"Reckon we can cut through?" Greene wondered.

"Maybe, with bolt cutters and time." Redding raked his beard and gazed out the single window.

"What're you thinking?" Blue asked.

Redding paced to the oculus and studied the blinding snow. "I've got an idea," he said. "But I don't think anyone's gonna like it."

Blue assumed he knew where Redding was headed.

"Mr. Duncan. In your expert opinion, how long do you think this storm will last?"

Duncan sighed through his nose. "Hard to tell. Could be hours. Could be days."

"Days," repeated Redding. "We don't have days."

Blue folded his arms. "You're thinking about the plane, aren't you?"

"I've got a hunch," Redding began, "that one of the bodies on that bird has the card."

"Christ," Domino groaned. "You're not suggesting we go back out?"

"Not suggesting." Redding held up a thick finger, his back still turned. "It's our only option."

"Or," Greene entered, "we can tuck tail and head back."

"We can't leave now, Mr. Greene. Not without seeing what's on the other end of that corridor." Redding faced the group. "I'm not asking anyone to come, but I'm going."

The wind screamed around the building.

"I'll go," Blue said. Everyone faced him. "I'll go," he said again.

Redding contemplated. "All right, Mr. Jennings."

"Blue," Domino began, "you can't."

Blue gazed into her eyes. "I have to."

"Then I'm going, too."

"Negative," Redding grunted. "We're the fastest two on this team. And in this weather, we can't afford to take our time."

"Blue, what're you thinkin'?" Greene exploded. "It's lookin' like the Everest storm of '96!"

Blue was more interested in Duncan's opinion, but the old man bit his tongue.

Redding unwrapped the climbing rope from around him and told Blue to don a harness. "We're gonna hold ourselves accountable, Mr. Jennings," he said, cinching the rope around himself. "If one goes down, we both go down."

"Fair enough," Blue replied, knotting the other end of the rope to the handle.

"You can't do this," Domino said again. "It's suicide."

Blue placed both hands on her shoulders. "I'll be fine. I promise."

"Come back," Domino whispered. "Don't leave me to die with Greene."

"Never," he winked. "No one else is gonna die."

"You set, Mr. Jennings?" Redding asked, zipping his jacket up.

"Let's go."

The wind hammered the bunker entry. It took both men to push it open, but they managed to slip through. Before it closed, Blue took one last look.

Duncan watched him with a disapproving look. Blue understood.

It was one of the worst storms Blue had ever known. The cold was blanching, the snow so blinding he could hardly see his hand. He had been swallowed by countless blizzards on Everest, but this somehow felt his first.

With his left hand, Blue clenched the rope as Redding led the way. He buried his face into the crook of his other arm, desperate to conceal all skin from the knifing frost.

He wasn't sure how Redding knew exactly where to go. The man must have a good memory, because they got there with remarkable speed. Redding untied the rope from around him and ordered Blue to wait outside as he searched the plane.

Blue crouched under the wing, taking cover against the wind. He surveyed the wreckage, guilty to wish that Stone's body had been among the others.

Suddenly, the ground began to rumble. At first, Blue feared an earthquake. It felt like the galloping of a hundred horses.

He ate the land with his eyes. The scope was still murky, but still he scanned frenetically, hoping he could find an answer to ease his mind. He could not, however, for the rumbling ceased.

Redding appeared and pulled Blue into a copse of debris.

"Did you find it?" Blue screamed.

Redding grinned victoriously, and handed him a silver card. "Here it is!"

Blue pocketed the key card as Redding reconnected them.

"Let's go!" Redding started, pulling Blue along.

He wanted to tell him about the rumbling, but figured it could wait. All he wanted was to get back inside.

He gripped the rope and slugged onward, his arm guarding his face once more. His teeth began to chatter, and he hoped Redding couldn't hear his discomfort over the wind.

As they pushed on, the ground trembled again. It was stronger this time, closer than before. Whatever it was, it was heading their way.

Then Blue heard it: a low, guttural growl in the shade behind him. The tremors grew faster. He didn't want to look, but he forced himself.

Blue squinted into the sleet. Through the flurry, he could see what was stalking them. The shape of a quadrupedal behemoth bore down at him.

Blue froze, heart pummeling ribs. He went blank. Was this Redding's monster? He didn't have much time to think: the creature smacked into him with the force of a bus.

Blue hit the snow like a meteorite. He gasped for air, wauling in Redding's direction. "Look out!"

It was too late. The rope snapped taut, towing him forward like a ragdoll.

Through the tempest, he could hear Redding shrieking. The rope would stop, Redding would wrangle the beast, and the ride would continue once more.

Blue dug his boots into the slush and yanked the slack from the skirmish, trying to thwart the merciless rope.

"Cut the rope, Jennings!" he suddenly heard Redding shout. "Cut the goddamn rope, Blue!"

He stopped pulling. His mind wondered back to that day on Everest. The rope tight in his hand. The features of the cliff face. Adam dangling beneath him, dragging him into the void.

Redding screamed again, carting Blue from one nightmare to another.

He could not cut the rope.

The dragging ceased and Blue could stand. He scrambled up and stumbled forward cautiously. A snarl welled up and he crouched. Redding was lying on the ground.

Before he could reach him, the creature reappeared. It hulked above Redding, sniffing his unmoving body. Blue could only watch as a grapefruit-sized chunk of Redding's neck came off in the monster's maw.

Redding's screams gargled over. He grabbed at his face, his shoulders, his feet kicking into the gory snow.

Blue choked. "Redding!"

The creature spied Blue with fiery, runny eyes. Its mouth opened and Blue saw a thick row of chisels behind the bloody lips.

Redding did not concede. Despite the blood rapids of his neck, he continued to fight the beast. Hoisting Redding up with its jaws, it drove him into the snow over and over.

Redding gurgled and spluttered like a dove at the wrath of a cat. Red splattered about as the animal mauled him. Then, one final time, it smashed him into the ice and waited.

Redding lied lifelessly, his body broken like those in the wreckage. Grabbing his arm, the bear dragged him off.

Blue stood in shock, waiting to be pulled along again. Nothing happened. He knew why, but still reeled in the slackened rope.

He saw the frayed end and knew what Redding had done. Somehow, in the scuffle, the man had managed to sever the rope connecting them. This had no doubt saved Blue's life.

The storm raged but Blue did not feel the jaw-tightening cold. He stood in disbelief, unable to process what he had just seen. But the fact remained: he was alone.

A resonant roar in the distance curdled his skin. He needed to get moving. He did his best to remember which way was correct, and he broke into a sprint.

Fifteen

Stone's camp appeared in the haze like a ship through the fog. Blue had depleted all reserve strength. Exhausted, he made his way to the doorway and burst inside the bunker.

He collapsed to his knees, but a pair of arms caught him before he could fall entirely.

"Blue!" Domino's voice cut into his ears. "What happened? What's wrong?"

"Redding!" he shivered. "It took him!"

Duncan bent down. "What?"

"A giant polar bear!" He knew it sounded crazy. "Killed Redding. Dragged him off!"

"Redding's dead?" Duncan stepped back.

Greene flew to the window, searching through the flurry.

"Did you see it?" Domino whispered.

"Ripped him up like a lion." He wept with abandon.

Domino ran her fingers through his bushy hair. She shushed him, and placed her forehead on his.

"We gotta get outta here!" Greene yelled. "We can't stay here no more. Forget Hayes and Redding! Forget Stone! This shit has gone ass-backwards."

Duncan agreed. "This is out of hand. Two deaths is enough for me to call it quits." He listened to the storm. "I say when this clears, we run for it."

Blue shook his head. "No," he sniffed. "You don't know what's out there."

Domino looked up. "He needs time," she told Duncan.

"We've got some," he reminded them, "but Doska is leaving in a few hours. I don't know about you but I am not getting left in the middle of nowhere."

Blue mumbled something no one quite heard.

"What?" Domino asked.

Blue removed the silver card and tossed it onto the concrete. "We reached the plane," he said. "We got the card."

Greene scoffed. "That don't matter now."

Blue sat up and glared at him severely. "Redding died for this, and I'll be damned if it was for nothing."

"This *is* all for nuthin'!" Greene erupted. "Dr. Stone is dead! Half the team is dead! We ain't got a debt to pay no more."

Duncan ignored Greene. "What do you want to do, Blue?"

Blue rose sluggishly. "Find out what's on the other side of this door." He retrieved the card and shuffled to the secret passage, careless who followed.

Taking his flashlight out, he assessed the descent with hesitation. He thought of the bear, afraid of what other nightmares might be hidden in the depths.

Before he could second-guess himself, the team stacked up behind him.

"We got your back, Blue," Duncan said. "We're in this together."

Blue nodded, looking from Duncan to Domino to Greene. "Keep your eyes open," he warned. He stepped through the archway and started on down.

When Blue swiped the card at the gate, the red light stopped flashing and turned a stalwart green. A metallic *click* was heard, and Blue gently pushed against the links.

The door swung open and he stepped forward. "Stay close," Blue said.

On both sides of the corridor were dilapidated prison cells. The bars were muscular like the cage upstairs, but the interiors were smaller, like it was meant for humans. There was no bedding in them, however, just rusted buckets containing a godawful, prehistoric stench.

Domino shined her light in one of the cells and whistled. "Hell of a place to do time," she remarked.

"Y'all reckon why this place is built lower than a snake's belly in a wagon rut?" Greene said to no one in particular.

Blue paid no mind to the chambers. He was focused on the steel door ahead. He walked quickly, Duncan hot on his heels. He was determined now. He knew they were close to the answer they'd been searching for.

The bulkhead door had a square window at the top, similar to the size of a porthole. He snared the rusty handle, but it was locked. Blue stood on his toes and tried to see through, but the room on the other side was dark.

"Another card scanner," Duncan observed.

Blue followed his gaze and saw a similar mechanism like the one at the previous gate. He gently swiped the card and waited. No *click* this time; the door remained locked.

"Goddammit!" Blue yelled, slamming his fist against the door.

"We gave it our best shot," Greene said, unconcerned.

Blue placed his head against the cold steel. "Please," he whispered to himself. "There's gotta be a way." He glanced up at the deteriorated hinges connecting the door to the wall. "Greene, you still got the ice pick?"

Greene hauled his backpack around and pulled out the tool. "This is about as useful as a pogo stick in quicksand, Blue," he grumbled.

Blue gripped the pick tightly and wedged the sharp end in the weakened part of the top hinge. With all his strength he pushed the pick upward and popped the joint off. It clanged to the ground, whereupon he went to the other.

"This could work," Duncan said.

"It will work." Blue kept chipping away at the door's framework. When he had stripped away the connecting metal, he took a step back and kangaroo-kicked the door.

To his surprise, he felt it weaken. Duncan noticed this and braced himself against it. "Let's push," he suggested.

They lunged at the door like twin battering rams. The framework scraped against the archway. It was only a matter of time.

"It's gonna give!" Duncan shouted.

One final time, they threw themselves at the door and it collapsed inward. They fell inside and Blue struggled to his feet.

Domino and Greene tiptoed in. The room was pitch black; the emerald light from the corridor offered no help. Blue removed his flashlight and checked the walls for a light switch. Instead, he found a breaker box and swept over the switches.

They were all in the off position. Blue didn't know which ones were the lights, so he flipped them all on.

Suddenly, a row of piercing fluorescent beams above illumed the room. Blue spun around and took in the sight.

It was a laboratory, very similar to how Blue had always pictured the compound. Wooden tables were arranged throughout, topped with microscopes, vials of rosy liquid, and papers—reams and reams of paper.

They spread out and examined the lab. The stench of the room reeked with a mix of cleaning supplies and something that smelled like excrement. There was also quite a bit of water puddled on the ground. Blue tried to ignore this and picked up one of the scattered documents: log reports with numbers and diagrams charting past experiments.

"What do you make of that?" Duncan studied from over his shoulder.

Blue shook his head in amazement. "Dr. Stone was doing some serious work down here."

Greene shouted from the other side of the lab. Another bulkhead access door—the exact design as one they had just broken down—was the only other route they could see. This one, however, did not have a window. Instead, a sliding hatch was built diagonally across the middle axis.

Greene put his hand on the handle and was about to push when a scurrying from the corner of the room stopped everyone in their tracks. Blue turned to the direction of the sound and stared, waiting. His heart began to thump rapidly and his breathing hastened. The sound was too small to be the colossal creature he encountered earlier. But his mind still raced with dreadful curiosity.

Another shuffle. Blue motioned for everyone to stay back and slunk toward the sound. It was coming from under a desk wedged in the corner.

Spotting a scalpel on a nearby table, he palmed it and pressed on. The shuffling gave way to whimpering. As he stood above the desk, he found the source of the noise. It was not an animal, but a human.

A human male.

In one swift motion, Blue slid away the desk and arced his weapon in the air. He jumped back immediately, however, startled to find a man curled into a ball, his knees locked against his chest.

"My God," Blue murmured. He tossed the scalpel and tried to absorb what he saw.

The man gazed up in delirium, squinting against the lights.

It didn't take long for Blue to recognize him.

It was Dr. Stone.

Sixteen

Blue had never seen a man so bewildered. Stone retreated further into the corner, shielding his face with clammy hands.

Blue faced the group. "It's Stone!" he called out. He bent down as the group rushed over. "It's okay, Dr. Stone!" he gently said. "It's going to be all right."

The others stood a few steps back, gazing in astonishment.

Greene looked like he was going to be sick. "Well, shut my mouth."

"Dr. Stone!" Duncan said. "Don't be afraid. We're not here to hurt you. Your wife sent us."

Stone slowly put his hands down. "Heather," he muttered. "Heather…"

Blue looked at Domino. Together, they pushed the desk away, uncovering Stone from his hiding place. Domino got to her knees, pulling a canteen from her pack. Stone grabbed it straightaway and gulped the remaining water. He breathed heavily, studying the gawking faces.

"Who are you people?" he trembled.

Blue squatted next to Domino. "I'm Blue Jennings," he said. "That's Duncan, Greene and Domino." He pointed to everyone quickly. "Your wife, the Governor, hired us to come find you and your team."

Stone nodded, chest heaving like the sea. "My team!" he said. "Are they okay? Are they still here?" He looked from Blue to Duncan.

"I'm sorry, Dr. Stone," Duncan replied. "They didn't make it."

Stone sighed. He swept his hand over his bald head and stared off into space. "Are all of them..."

Domino placed her hand on his. Stone buried his head in his lap and wept.

"It wasn't supposed to happen like this," he cried. "We had everything under control! Everything!"

"What happened here, Dr. Stone?" Blue pressed. He knew now may not be the time to ask, but he wasn't going to wait around for answers.

"And what exactly *is* this place?" Greene added.

Stone began to recover and rubbed his eyes with his dirty white shirt. "Guess it's pointless to keep this all a secret." He sat up, and Blue helped him to his feet. "I assume you've seen the whole facility, correct?"

"We've seen the holding cells and the giant cages," Domino replied.

Blue wanted to tell him about the bear but decided to wait.

Stone staggered to another desk, using the neighboring tables for support. "This place used to be a prison of sorts for spies during the Cold War. Our government would bring people up here and torture the hell out of them. It was like our very own gulag." Stone opened one of the drawers and tossed a file onto the table. Blue splashed over and opened it, thumbing through the pages.

Some of them contained typed reports with words that had been redacted in black ink. But he noticed that they were all being sent to the same man.

A man called Mr. Young.

"Young," he said to himself, thinking about the gray man on Everest. He doubted it was a coincidence.

He continued to riffle through the documents until he reached photographs. They were black and white, but Blue could still see the grisly images of prisoners going through myriad forms of torture. He was about to close the file, when something caught his eye: a subject in every photo inflicting pain on each suspect. He examined the face closer.

At first he didn't believe it. He thought the cold was cheating his vision. But the piercing eyes were a dead giveaway. The beard. It was unmistakable.

The man was Dave Redding.

"No way," Blue gasped. "This can't be." He held the photos out for the team.

"I'll be damned," Duncan said, flummoxed.

Greene spat. "That snake in the grass."

Domino couldn't believe it. "The secret door," she murmured. "He knew about this place."

"You know this man?" Stone questioned.

Blue nodded slowly. "His name is Redding. He came up here with us."

"Where is he now?"

Blue turned away. "Some giant bear took him."

Stone's eyes widened. "Pandora."

"Pandora?" Greene echoed.

"Yes," Stone fumbled around again in the drawer. He pinched another file and handed it to Blue. "Pandora is a polar bear, or some type of one anyhow."

Duncan read the file with Blue. "What do you mean?"

Stone exhaled. "Let's go back fifteen years," he began. "I was assigned a flight as Commander of the Space Shuttle, *Vanguard*, the newest vehicle in the fleet. Our mission was to capture an oncoming satellite and bring it back to Earth."

"An oncoming satellite?" said Domino. "Was it coming down?"

"No, it was returning from deep space," Stone explained. "And when I say satellite, I actually mean robot."

"A space robot?" drawled Greene.

"Indeed. The robot was named *Clementine*, a new vehicle designed by some of the smartest minds on the planet. It's thought that, long ago after the Big Bang, comets and asteroids containing ice crashed into Earth. A popular hypothesis says this is why there's water on Earth.

"Most asteroids in our Solar System are in a limbo orbit around a place known as the asteroid belt. Right in the middle of two orbiting planets, Mars and Jupiter, this

debris field can be scattered anywhere at any time.
Scientists have wanted to launch a spacecraft to one of
these objects and collect samples for study. They didn't
want to risk anything burning up in the atmosphere upon
reentry, so they planned to capture it before Earth's gravity
sucked it back in.

"Which is where my mission comes in. It was a
toilsome task, but I was a career astronaut, this being my
fifth ride into space. No one could fly a shuttle better than
me. Which came to a surprise to everyone at NASA, myself
included, when I botched it."

"You missed it?" said Blue.

"My math was off. We practiced the capture for two
and a half years, ever since the *Clementine* launch. But I *still*
miscalculated the trajectory by a few miles." He grunted at
this recollection. "That's something that should only ever
happen in a simulator. It still haunts me; I will never stop
seeing *Clementine* zipping past us." Stone paused and took a
deep breath, but moved on. "Fast forward two weeks.
NASA's survey team tracked its crash landing up here in
the Arctic, which is when we started our search on foot. It
took us a few days, but we finally found it—well, *I* did.
Clementine had crashed into the side of this very crater, into
a pool of water blocking the entrance to a cave. But as we
began to clean up the *Clementine* wreckage, we realized it
wasn't a cave at all; it was a den."

Blue raised his eyebrows. "A bear den."

"Correct," Stone replied. "Two small cubs, couldn't
have been more than a few days old, crawled out towards
us." He smiled, holding everyone's gaze. "They seemed to
be normal pups. We couldn't just leave them there. If their
mother was still alive, she would have been there. So we
took them with us." He spread his arms out. "To this
facility. And that's when things started to get weird."

"Weird," Blue echoed. "How so?"

"'Weird' may not be scientific, but that's the best
way to say it. I remember holding one of the cubs. Its eyes
were still shut, but as I was scratching the top of its head,
they opened and looked up." Stone stopped. "They were
red, bright red, a carmine red. I knew it was odd, so I
checked the other cub. Same eyes." He shook his head. "At

the time, I didn't think much of it. I didn't know a damn thing about polar bears. We also had *Clementine* to study and repair while we were here. So we put the two cubs in a single cage and let them be."

"Why didn't your team just take *Clementine* and go home?" Domino asked. "Why keep it up here?"

"A couple years before all this happened, NASA partnered with an environmental company called Global Ethos. Some contractors from GE were up here already, studying possible reasons for the melting ice caps. NASA had also loaned them a bunch of mechanical equipment at the time. My guess is they wanted to build a secret launch facility up here."

Duncan chuckled. "In Santa's backyard?"

Stone shrugged. "The Cold War was a strange time." He cleared his throat. "Global Ethos had the tools up here we could use to take *Clementine* apart and extract the asteroid samples. But days into our research, our attention turned elsewhere."

"The cubs," Blue said.

Stone stared off at the gradually flooding floor. "It was the strangest thing. In the course of forty-eight hours, the cubs grew from the size of a kitten to the size of a tiger." He looked back at Blue. "And they were aggressive. Meanest animals I've ever crossed."

Greene stopped him. "In two days, they grew *that* big? How'd you reckon that?"

"Well," Stone said, "that's why I've spent the better part of a decade up here."

"You're an astronaut and an engineer," said Blue. "Why was it your business to study these bears?"

Stone took a seat at the desk and held his shiny head. For a moment, he stared at the cluttered table, thinking hard about his next words.

Finally, he spoke. "Do you believe in aliens?"

Greene let out a nervous hoot. "You ain't about to say what I think you're gonna say?"

Stone stared back at him, puncturing his naivety.

"All right, Dr. Stone, one damn second," Duncan declared. "You're not about to tell us aliens are *real* and somehow involved in all this?"

"When most people think of extraterrestrial life, they think of UFOs zooming around the sky, or skinny, gray lizard people snatching humans in the night for experimentation. But the logical hypothesis, at least in my line of work, is that tiny forms of bacteria exist outside of Earth, and can possibly be found on planets or NEOs that contain water. Near-Earth objects, that is.

"For example, one of Jupiter's moons, Europa, is mostly ice. NASA and other space enthusiasts believe that there is life underneath all that ice. Because where we've found water, we've found fathomable existence."

Blue peered at Domino. She seemed skeptical; this was something she wouldn't buy easily.

"So why the asteroid?" she demanded. "Why not just send *Clementine* to this moon?"

"Financially, a mission like that would cost an arm and a leg, especially for a hypothesis based off such a shot-in-the-dark speculation. Some NEO hunters and higher-ups at NASA figured the best way, at the time, was to wait for an asteroid to come within close proximity to Earth, then have a spacecraft land on it."

"Sounds like one hell of a rodeo," said Greene.

Stone agreed. "The human mind is an incredible thing."

Blue dove into the files again. "Tell us about the samples."

Stone closed his eyes. "One of the ice samples contained bacteria with constantly alternating light and dark colors. We discovered that the cells began to multiply, which made the object heavier." He opened his eyes. "Which explained why I miscalculated the trajectory; *Clementine* became heavier over time because of this constant duplication. And that's where the polar bears come into play."

Blue began to piece the puzzle together. "Dr. Stone, you're theorizing that these bears, combined with the bacterial residue, are now some kind of alien mutant?"

"A theory would make it true," Stone told everyone. "So I guess it's time to make it official."

Greene slid off his desk and landed in the freezing sea water. "Can't believe this goddamn rescue mission be turnin' into this shit! I ain't deserve none of this! I climb mountains for a livin'! If I knew what this woulda turned into, I woulda never signed on!"

The group paid him no mind, yet the thought was mutual.

"Who else knows about this?" Duncan uttered.

Stone shrugged again nonchalantly. "Me, my team, and I guess my superior and his guys."

Duncan approached Stone's desk. "Does this bacterium transfer to humans?" he said, concerned.

"We never got to human trials," Stone said, "but in my ten years of research, we've found that airborne exposure cannot cross over."

"What about other animals?" Blue asked.

"We found that rats and monkeys can contract the bacteria by drinking contaminated water."

Domino rested hands on hips. "So where are these experiments now?"

"Dead. All except for one."

"Pandora," Blue hissed.

"Yes."

"So which one of the cubs is Pandora?" Domino wanted to know.

Stone bit his lip. "Well, Pandora is actually the *offspring* of the two cubs."

"They got busy?" Greene exclaimed.

Stone nodded. "We had them in the same cage. We didn't think much about it. A few years passed, then all of a sudden, out pops this third cub."

Blue continued to flip through the second file. "Was this one different?"

"Her eyes were the same, deep red, but she was far more violent than the others. She also grew *twice* as fast as they did, which to remind you, was already unnaturally quick."

Domino brushed her bangs to the side. "How did the other bears die?"

Stone smirked. "She ate them."

"Jesus," said Greene.

"And she kept growing. The cage we had her in became too small." He pointed to the unopened door on the other side of the lab. "There's an old cargo elevator in there that we used to transport her down. We converted that room into her new holding cell, and for the last five or so years, that's where she's been contained."

"So how the hell did she get out?" Blue asked, noticing the doorways were far too small for a creature that size to fit through.

Stone pointed upward. "Above us is water. We are nine stories under the ice. About a week ago, she broke through the ceiling, flooded the room, and swam out."

The four explorers turned to the bulkhead.

"That entire room is filled with water?" Duncan looked back.

"I wouldn't open it if I were you," advised Stone.

Domino leaned back against a table. "So, that's how you got trapped in here?"

Frowning, Stone stood from the chair. "It happened so fast. My team was on the other side of the lab near Pandora's chamber. Something had been going on with her; she was more hostile than usual. After compromising the roof, she kept pushing against the door and I was afraid she would break through." He turned his attention to the sliding hatch on the bulkhead. "That was wide open and a member of my team, Andrew Bradly, rushed to close it. That's when Pandora bit into his arm and literally tore it out of the socket."

His eyes glassed over. "As they attended to him, I rushed to hold the door. I guess they figured me for dead, because they ran out and locked it behind them."

Domino held him with compassion. "They abandoned you, Dr. Stone?"

"No," he asserted. "They are good men. It wasn't like that."

Duncan broke the news about how they left in the plane. "They were killed in the crash."

Stone scoffed loudly and put his head down. "None of them even knew how to fly the damn thing. That was our way out."

"We've got a boat, Dr. Stone," Blue responded. "About an hour or so from here."

Stone eyed him closely. "We wouldn't make it. Not while she's out there."

"Why didn't y'all kill the beast!" Greene yelled, getting to his feet. "It was obviously outta control from the get-go!"

"You clearly know nothing about science," Stone replied coldly. "We are not going to smite what could be the greatest scientific discovery of our time."

"Well," Greene continued, "your Nobel Peace Prize is fixin' on the warpath."

"If you were in my shoes, Mr. Greene, you would have done exactly the same thing."

Greene pursed his lips tightly.

Duncan stepped away and began to search the lab. "Do you have any kind of weapons in here?"

"Of course not," Stone puffed.

"Well I don't mean to rush you, Doc, but we're on a time frame," Duncan said, ransacking a drawer.

Stone faced Blue. "What does he mean?"

Blue replied, "Our captain gave us till nightfall to find you. If we weren't back in time, he'd leave without us."

"I see there wasn't a lot of confidence in my survival," Stone said thinly.

"Tim Hayes believed you were still alive," Domino blurted.

"Tim Hayes is here?" Stone said with raised brows. "Is he on the ship?"

"He came here with us," Blue explained, "to the compound."

Stone grinned. "So he's topside then?"

This time, Domino broke the news. "He fell through the ice," she said. "We don't believe he made it."

Stone kept a stony face. Blue was going to console him, but then Stone began to walk. He waded through the pooling water, stopping just shy of the closed bulkhead.

"His daughter..." Stone trailed off.

"I know," Domino mourned.

Blue could sympathize. He knew he felt accountable for Hayes' death. Blue gleaned that Stone was coming to one conclusion: he was going to have to cope with this forever. It was discomfiting to watch.

It did not last, however. A startling bang came from the other side of the steel. Originally, Blue thought Stone had thrown something against it. But as the doctor slowly backed away, Blue realized there was only one thing it could be.

Dr. Stone stared at them in trepidation. "She's here."

Seventeen

The door would not hold for long. Ice-cold water spewed in tiny rivulets around the frame as Blue and Greene rushed to stem it.

Stone began darting from table to table, swiping files and other research. Duncan caught up and slapped the papers away.

"We gotta go!" He clamped Stone's arm and dragged him back to the corridor.

"Let me go!" Stone struggled. "I'll lose everything!"

"It's not worth your life!" Duncan protested.

"It *is* my life!"

"Forget what he says, get him up top!" Blue ordered. His back strained against the heavy door, his calves burning from keeping the elements at bay.

The bang returned, rattling their bones. More Arctic water sprayed out, drenching the men. They weren't going to last much longer.

Domino stood between the two groups. Her head moved from them to the exit. Blue recognized her deer-in-headlights posture; he had the same reaction when he first encountered Pandora.

"Go! Help Duncan!" Blue grunted.

Her eyes pleaded with him and she shook her head quickly.

"Now!" he shouted. "We'll be right behind you!"

Domino gave him one last glance and then made for the hallway.

They were strong, he and Greene. Decades of climbing had given them superhuman leg muscles. But they were no match for the crushing pressure and the unrelenting beast.

A *ping* rung from the top hinge of the door. Then another. Greene looked at him; they both knew they were out of time.

"No use beatin' a dead horse!" Greene shouted, turning his head from a jet of water. "Go on! Save yourself!"

Despite the perilous situation, Blue managed a smile. "What, and let you take all the credit?"

Greene returned the grin. Blue wasn't sure why, but Greene's gigantic teeth seemed whiter than they ever had before. He opened his mouth to drawl out something witty, but before he could speak, the door gave way.

It collapsed inwards on Greene's side first and Blue had just a split second longer to jump away. Greene, leaning in with his shoulder, was swept underneath the door as a cascade of freezing sea poured into the lab.

Blue was knocked on his back, and the current ferried him all the way to the corridor. Straining upward, he snagged a table and hauled himself to his feet. He was safe for the moment. It was Greene, however, who concerned him.

Blue cupped his hands around his mouth. "Greene!" he shouted over the roar, but there was no reply. He attempted to push forward, but the oncoming flow kept him at bay. "Greene!" he cried out once more.

An arm reached out from the doorway. Blue could see the rest of Greene's body trapped under the weight of the door. Greene was drowning.

Jumping on a nearby table, he skipped across the tops of desks and other objects, avoiding the sweeping current. When he reached Greene, he splashed fearlessly into the water and heaved with all his might.

The bulkhead didn't budge. It was wedged against something down below and Blue didn't have time to find out what it was. Instead, he grabbed Greene's arm and tugged.

Slowly, more and more of Greene's body emerged from the water. His head finally reached the surface and he gasped loudly for air.

"Holy shit!" He drew long, deep lungfuls from the damp air. "I was gonna say...I'm more nervous than a long tailed cat…in a room full of rocking chairs. What took ya so long?"

Blue got him to his feet and they stood together on the door, just to the side of the relentless torrent.

Greene was recovering when Blue suddenly noticed the pressure subsiding. Something was blocking the entrance. Something very big.

He turned to look at Greene just in time to see Pandora's enormous snout thrust through the opening. In one swift motion, it snapped its jaws around Greene's head, then pulled him into the flooded room.

Blue was so shocked, he never felt the blood-soaked water pressure blast him away. He let the current sweep him hard into a wall, scarcely registering the frigor. He couldn't move. He gazed unblinking at a table surging towards him, and waited.

It slammed into him, pinning his arms to his side and body to the wall. The pain snapped him back to reality, and he desperately found himself fighting an unwinnable fight. The water was nearly up to his neck. It wouldn't be long.

Maybe this is a good thing, Blue thought. He looked up, keeping his chin above the water. He watched the lights flicker, then go dark, bathing him in blackness. He closed his eyes and waited.

Another force struck the desk, but it wasn't the water. The pressure released his arms, and he slipped them free. With the heels of his hands, he pushed the table up and he snaked from his would-be wooden tomb.

A hand grabbed his jacket sleeve and pulled him along with the current. The water sucked them towards the corridor and spat them out into the quickly flooding hallway.

The emerald light still shone, and through the dimness, Blue could discern his savior.

"Domino," he panted.

Her bangs stuck to her forehead and she tried, unsuccessfully, to purse her lips to an angle where she could blow them away. "Couldn't leave without you, slick," she said coolly.

Blue stood, eyes feral with fear. "Greene...he...he's gone..."

Domino grabbed his wrist and pulled him towards the stairs. "We won't be next," she assured him.

They reached the top and continued on. Domino towed him past the giant cage, around the severed arm, through the room with the machine parts, and out onto the ice.

To Blue's surprise, the storm had receded. The sun, however, was beginning to set. Doska would leave soon, and Blue knew they had to hustle.

In the distance, Duncan and Stone were starting the trek up the inside lip of the crater. They were making good time, but they had to hurry to catch up.

Domino looked ahead. "You up for a little run?"

Blue kicked the snow. "Let's go."

They flew through the freshly powdered snow, following the pair of footsteps. Blue occasionally glanced behind, making sure Pandora wasn't in tow. Despite the minor ice cracks accumulating underfoot, they were safe.

For the moment.

They reached the slope of the crater, but didn't catch their breaths. Domino kept pulling Blue along; what she lacked in speed she more than compensated in endurance.

He slipped on the icy rocks. A few times he fell, but Domino pulled him back up.

"C'mon, Blue!" she shouted. "Don't give up on me now, dammit!"

"Never," he wheezed.

Duncan and Stone awaited them at the hilltop. When they reached the summit, Blue collapsed and searched the sea for the *Busefal*.

In the orange-red glow of the setting sun, he spotted the vessel in the water. Blue sighed and flopped the rest of the way to the blackened sands.

"Mr. Greene?" Duncan said to him.

Blue shook his head.

Dr. Stone put his head down and turned from the camp. "I'm sorry."

"We can do this later," Domino interrupted. "But we are getting off this island."

A distant, thundering *crack* turned everyone's attention back to the compound. Stone gazed down into the crater.

"Pandora?" Duncan asked.

"No," replied Stone. "Gravity."

White foam sprayed from large openings around the ice. The compound wobbled and tilted back and forth. Everyone watched in dismay as the hangar went under first, then the bunker, disappearing beneath a thick, snowy shroud.

Stone was defeated. "Where did we go wrong? This could have been…"

Duncan knelt beside him. "C'mon, Dr. Stone. We got a lovely lady that's been waiting to see you."

Stone sniffled, taking one last look at the sinking crater. "Take me home," he said.

They descended the rope on the other end of the hillside. Blue didn't bother to take the anchors back out; they weren't worth the extra energy.

When they returned to the ice pack, Duncan searched for the markers they had previously placed. But they were nowhere in sight.

"The storm took 'em," he concluded. "Everyone stay behind me."

The sun nearly dipped behind the horizon. The ice reflected the sky's final fiery light, bathing the route before them in a canvas of bright colors. It was one of the prettiest views Blue had ever witnessed. *The butterfly of Siberia,* he thought. *Noah's dove.*

The horn blasted across the tundra. Blue watched the *Busefal* for a long time, trying to figure out if he spotted someone waving from the deck.

"I wonder what Doska will make of all this?" Blue said to Domino.

"We got Stone," she responded. "I doubt he cares about anything else."

"Hey," Blue stopped her. "About what happened back there. I just wanted to say—"

"You're welcome," she finished for him. "But it's gonna cost you."

"What's the damage?"

Domino pulled him close. "I want you to be honest with me. About what happened to Adam. I want you to tell me the truth."

Blue knew the time had come. He had to face the evil that plagued his mind; answer for his committed crime that borderlined murder. There was no more road for him to run. It was time for the truth.

"Adam...I killed him," he said. Then he looked at her. "I let him die."

"What?" she said. "But you said—"

Without warning, the ice began to fail around them. Blue snagged Domino by the wrist and pulled her away towards Duncan and Stone.

"Watch your feet!" he warned.

A large chunk of ice dipped into the water. It slanted in the air, a ponderous counterweight on the opposite end.

And then the first of Pandora's colossal paws launched from the abyss.

"You've gotta be kidding me!" Domino yelled out.

Blue spun around and pumped his arm toward the ship. "Go!" his voice echoed across the pack.

But the ice continued to break. Suddenly, they found themselves cut off from the ship, stranded on a singular floe with the beast.

The ice surprisingly held. When Pandora loomed from the water, Blue, for the first time in his third encounter, was able to see the beast in its entirety. It was just how Redding described it: the elephantine creature wobbled forward, glaring at them with dead eyes.

Blue stood between the bear and the group. Pandora growled in their direction.

"Stay behind me," Blue said quietly.

No one moved as the bear approached. Pandora's lips curled back, revealing rotting chisels. She panted harshly, sniffing the air.

Suddenly, she leapt back onto her hind legs. Blue craned his neck back as Pandora roared into the darkening sky. The ice shook violently as her front paws pounded the ice.

Everyone but Blue lost their balance. He stayed firmly planted, his eyes on the bear. He knew if he didn't do something, their lives would be wasted. All this for nothing.

They had come too far.

"Don't do it," Domino said from the ground. "Don't you do something stupid, slick, I mean it." Her voice broke.

"Never," he whispered. Then he ran forward.

He didn't hear Domino calling after him. He didn't feel the ice cracking beneath his feet or Pandora's furnace-breath against his skin. He lowered his shoulder and charged.

When he hit the monster, his shoulder slid out of place and he was knocked to the ground. He ignored the flaring pain and attempted to right himself. He looked up just in time to see Pandora's clawed hand bearing down upon him.

The piercing tips of the claws slashed down the left side of his cheek and down his neck. Blue seized his throat, feeling the blood spurting through his fingertips.

Domino screamed from behind him, but another one of Pandora's bellows drowned out her cries. Blue looked up at his impending doom and spat bloody defiance into its fur.

"I'm ready!" he yelled.

Euphoria washed over him. All these years of watching people die first-hand; he had never taken the time to imagine his own death. He figured it would happen on Everest, not at the wrath of an alien polar bear.

Pandora sniffed him, drawing her head back to strike. Blue didn't turn away. He faced his doom with pride. He hoped it would be quick.

Before Pandora was about to crunch into him, her head was knocked away by another figure. At first, Blue thought it was Domino. He turned back to the group, surprised to see everyone accounted for.

Blue picked his head up from the ice and looked at Pandora. Mounted on her back covered in blood, eyes crazed like a madman, was Dave Redding.

It was like watching an attempt at riding a bull. Pandora stomped around the ice, trying desperately to buck Redding off. The ice around them cracked more, and Blue could feel himself slipping into the sea.

With Pandora distracted, Domino was able to sneak over and pull Blue away from the chaos.

"Blue, talk to me!" she cried, examining his wound.

Blue did not reply; he could not take his attention from Redding. His hands dug deep into her matted fur as he tossed about wildly. Pandora kept whipping her head back, snapping furiously at the human tick atop her neck.

Redding moved one hand up and unsheathed the knife on his jacket. The blade glimmered in the dying light before he brought it down savagely into her spine.

Pandora's wail rocked the frozen wasteland. She kicked about faster than before, direly trying to remove Redding. But he did not let up. He stabbed her over and over, each thrust angrier and angrier.

One of Pandora's paws burst through the ice and she collapsed on her stomach. Redding was knocked off her back, but recovered quickly. He dodged one chomp, then another. He held the beast's snout towards the ice and plunged the blade mechanically into her brain. Pandora whimpered in agony. She was no match for his speed.

Redding stopped for a moment and backed away. He looked at the bear with dull eyes, watched it take its final breaths.

One gurgled sigh. Then another, long, slow exhale. Pandora was finished.

Blue drifted in and out. Each time he awoke, he saw Redding.

Duncan tried to speak, but Redding held his hand up in reply. He made his way to Blue and knelt beside him with Domino.

A bloody cloth was wrapped tightly around his neck. He wheezed with every breath. But other than that, he looked satisfied.

Hoarsely, he said, "You've got some balls, Mr. Jennings." The knife was still in his hand, and he rested it on Blue's chest. Then he stood, looking at no one but Dr. Stone.

He nodded once.

Stone stared wide-eyed, unsure of what to say. But before anyone said anything, Redding whirled around and strode from the ship, out toward the wilderness, back into the unknown.

Noises and voices seemed further and further away, though Blue did not move away from his companions. Domino talked sweetly to him, but he could only see her lips moving. Then that, too, began to fade.

And Blue Jennings fell into a world of darkness.

Eighteen

When he woke, he was lying in a soft bed swaddled in a warm blanket. As his eyes adjusted to the world around him, a constant beep drilled his grogginess.

It didn't take long for him to realize he was in a hospital. He tried to sit up, but his neck stung mercilessly. He grazed the gauze on the wound and tried to speak.

"Dom…" he groaned. "Domino?"

"I'm afraid not," came a voice.

"Who's that?" he mumbled.

A figure moved to the foot of his bed. It took him a moment, but Blue slowly recognized the man.

"Mr. Colby," he mumbled.

Colby leaned against the footrest. "You've seen better days, Mr. Jennings."

"Where's Domino?" he demanded scratchily. "Where am I?"

"Easy," Colby calmed him. "You're safe. You're in a hospital in Seattle recovering from a plane accident."

Blue thought back. "No," he said. "Mr. Colby, we were attacked by a giant bear. An *alien* bear."

Colby shook his head. "No you weren't."

"Yes we—" Blue stopped himself. "Wait. You *knew.*"

Colby looked at him, expression unchanging.

"I know about your experiments," Blue spat out. "I know about the torture program."

"You know nothing," Colby replied. "And you have no proof."

"Redding was one of yours," Blue continued. "You sent him there to make sure we wouldn't find those files on Young."

Colby shrugged. "Speculation. Too bad Redding was a raving drunk, delusional about Arctic mutants." He clicked his tongue. "I suggest you don't become one of those people." He then held out an envelope. "Also, the Governor sends her regards. She is relieved to have her husband back and is excited to resume her time on the campaign trail." He concealed the letter.

Blue ignored his statement. "Where's Domino?" he commanded again. "What have you done with her?"

"The girl is safe; you have my word." Colby smiled. "But she works for us now."

"What does that mean?"

"It means keep your distance, Mr. Jennings," Colby warned. "Her safety relies on you keeping a low profile and your mouth shut. Do you think you can do that?"

Blue said nothing. He glared furiously at Colby, wishing like hell he had the strength to jump out of this bed and strangle him to death.

Colby pulled Redding's knife from his back pocket and flipped it over in his hands. "This was his most prized possession, the only thing he kept with him from his survival in Siberia. And he gave it to you."

"One day, I'll use to kill you," Blue hissed.

Colby laughed and pointed the sharp end at Blue. "You're a man of many talents, Mr. Jennings, but I don't think taking life is one of them."

"Guess you'll just have to wait and see."

Colby raised the knife, then drove it down in the bedding between Blue's legs. "Remember," he reminded him, "not a word."

"We'll be seeing each other again," Blue forewarned.

Colby clasped his hands together. "Then I'll be looking forward to it." And then he was gone.

After Colby departed, the rains came, and Blue watched something other than snow descend from the sky for the first time in months. But he could only think about Domino.

He held onto the knife closely, hiding it under his pillow when nurses would come to check in. That night, while he was turning it over in his hands, he felt something carved in the wooden hilt. He rubbed his thumb over the worn-down words and read aloud to himself: "Throw me to the wolves and I will return leading the pack."

As he turned this over in his mind, his door suddenly opened. Blue stuffed the blade under the covers, expecting to see a nurse, but was surprised to find that it was not.

Mr. Duncan, grinning from ear to ear, gaped heartily down at Blue. "You look damn close to a million bucks," he said.

Blue forced a smile. "Mr. Duncan, how'd you find me?"

He pulled up a seat next to the bed, dropping a rucksack on the ground. Blue explained Colby's visit, and the story about Domino working for them. Duncan mentioned that she disappeared when the *Busefal* docked in Barrow, and that she willingly got into a separate van upon arrival.

"She said she had someone to speak to," Duncan said. "Figured it was someone from your mountain."

"She said she wanted to do something new," Blue lamented. "Said she wouldn't leave without saying goodbye. We had unfinished business, Duncan. I'm afraid she left because I confessed to letting someone die. Someone she loved."

Duncan did not react to Blue's startling confession. He watched silently as tears trickled down Blue's face.

Blue stared at the wall across from him. "I just don't know what else to do. I don't even know where to look for her. I want to make this right. I *need* to make this right."

Duncan reached down into the backpack at his feet. "I know where we can start," he said.

"It's too dangerous to go looking," Blue sniffed. "Maybe I should just let her go, let all of this go."

"I won't let you make the same mistake I did," Duncan said, unzipping the pack. "Listen, I took some souvenirs from our expedition."

"Souvenirs?"

Duncan smiled and pulled out stacks of wrinkled paper. "Stone's research," he said proudly. "And the files on Young."

Blue grabbed the documents and looked around the room. "They'll kill you for this," he whispered.

"Kill *us*," Duncan grinned again. "We're in this together, remember? This shit ain't over, not by a long mile."

Blue squeezed the papers tightly. "I told Colby I'd come for him. They'll be expecting us."

"Then we'll need a new team," Duncan said. "Got any ideas?"

Blue looked at the old man. "A few," he said.

"Good." Duncan leaned back. "We best get to work."

Blue took out Redding's knife and again read over the inscription. Redding gifted this to him for a reason; he had *earned* his survival. He had to keep moving forward. His story was not over.

"We're going to need people we can trust," Blue said. "I know just where to start."

Acknowledgements

This book would not have been possible without the many people who believed in me along the way. I'd like to give a special thanks to my editor, Evan Chiovari, who spent countless hours reading through the many stages of this book. I'd like to thank my artist, Gabi Esteban, for the beautiful cover art. As far as creative inspiration, I'd like to thank the following works: *Into Thin Air* by Jon Krakauer, *The Kid Who Climbed Everest* by Bear Grylls, *In the Kingdom of Ice* by Hampton Sides. There are a few others who gave me strength along the way. I shall list them now:
Jevel Williams, Vince Tolentino, Jeff Hester, Adam Kelley, Clementine Leger, Brad Mucha, Andrew Boesch, Teal Bowser, Robbie Carter, the Enzian Crew, Lane Cashdollar, the staff of Austin's Coffee, Gordon Folkes, Jay Olson and the rest of the Olson family, the Gillis Court gang, Michael Freeman, Merrill Frailey, the Killingsworth family, Lisa Laustsen, Alex Confer, Ryan Fisher, the creators of the Walking Dead (especially Andrew Lincoln), Tom Hanks and Emma Watson (just because) and of course, my mother, Abby Brown.

Made in the USA
Middletown, DE
30 April 2017